CONTENTS

GRUMPY AS PUCK

The first book in a new romantic comedy series by *USA Today bestselling author* **Elizabeth Lynx about a hockey player who was anything but nice. When he needed the help of his teammate's sister, the sweet-as-pie local veterinarian, to save his dog, he wondered if his secret crush from the past might be more than puppy love.**

My teammates called me Grumpy Old Man.

I understood the grumpy part. It wasn't as if I was the life of the party. But I wasn't old. Geez, I was only thirty-two.

Despite the only partly correct nickname, there's two things you needed to know about me. The first, I loved my dog and would do anything for that crazy mutt.

The second thing, well, it involved my teammates' sister. The woman he told me to stay away from. What nobody knew was I have had a crush on her for years.

Why was I telling you that?

My dog was in an accident and the only one who could save him? You guessed it. My secret crush was the local veterinarian.

What did I do to thank her? I got her fired. Now my secret crush thought I was a grumpy jerk too.

1

DAISY

The warm, gooey Szechuan chicken soaked through my shoes, and my toes wiggled in disgust at the sensation. But the sliminess of the spicy food leaking through my socks was a welcomed feeling from the shattering heartbreak of watching my boyfriend, buck naked, of the past two years explain to me that it was a good thing he was sleeping with my boss Angelica.

To Angelica's credit, she was wise enough not to add to the conversation as she sat next to him on our bed in only her birthday suit.

"Daisy, just hear me out." He held up his hands as if to stop me from bolting, which I wanted to do.

But I lived here too. And as much as I wanted to dash out the door and never look back, I was upset. That anger needed answers.

"Okay, I'm listening." I wiggled my toe and rubbed the clumps of chicken into his mother's Persian carpet.

She gave it to us when we moved in together last year. She told me she just knew I was the one, that she had a dream Andrew and I would be married one day.

I guess dreams never come true.

"So, you know how you've been tired lately... and we haven't had sex for a long time?"

I sucked in a breath and slid my gaze to my buxom boss. She yawned. I guess being caught sleeping with my boyfriend while learning about our pathetic sex life was tiring.

"Andrew, I don't want to talk about that right now. In fact, I want you both to leave." Folding my arms, I tapped my foot. It made a squishing sound as it pushed the food deeper into his mother's precious rug.

Andrew slid his fingers through his sandy blond hair. "But, Daisy, honey, I'm naked. Angelica... she's naked too." He waved at her as if I couldn't see her ridiculously curvy body—the type of body that belonged to a starlet from the Golden Age of Hollywood, not a veterinarian in a small mountain town.

"You're dressed." He gave me a sad smile. "If anyone should leave, it's probably you."

A pain shot through my chest, and my eyes burned. My god, I told him I loved him this morning before I grabbed my keys from our second-hand, chipped, wooden entrance table and headed out the door. Then I walked to work for that woman.

My eyes narrowed on her long black curls cascading over her sun-kissed shoulders. Stupidly, I was excited to prove to her that I'd make a great veterinarian one day.

What. An. Idiot.

The world felt off. My hand flew to my forehead. Was I about to faint? Ugh, that would be the cherry on top of the disappointment sundae that was my life.

Andrew would probably take me fainting as a compliment.

I couldn't believe this was actually happening to me. This was what happened in movies or soap operas, not in real life, and especially not in *my* life. I was the type of person who avoided conflict. I was the woman who did what she was told. A woman everyone liked because chaos wasn't part of my world.

In one night, all the crazy crap that had obviously been building over time spewed over me like the damn food covering my feet.

Word was going to get out, and it was only a matter of time before everyone would whisper about me. Gossip spreads like wildfire in small towns.

I knew what they would say. They'd call me pathetic while I worked for the woman who was banging my boyfriend.

If anyone was the sad one, it was Andrew. He had been unemployed for months, just sitting on our couch every day, refusing to go get a job. It wasn't the jobless part that bothered me; it was his lack of effort and doing nothing all day that wore me out.

At the very least, he could help around the apartment—cleaning and cooking so I wouldn't have to after work. Maybe even go to the grocery store just once. Any of that would have been helpful.

I stupidly thought it was a rough patch, and if I kept a positive attitude, it would help his confidence.

Someone was helping with his confidence, alright, but it wasn't me. My eyes bore into Angelica.

I had been the one to cook, clean, do the shopping, and work my ass off to prove to my boss that I would make an excellent partner at her veterinarian clinic. I was currently just an animal tech and only stepped in as a vet when she was off or had to leave early... like today.

"I hate to tell you, Angelica, but Andrew isn't a gynecologist."

Both of their brows crinkled in the dumbest way, and I sucked in my lips, trying not to laugh.

"What? I know he's not a doctor, Daisy. I'm not an idiot," she snorted.

"It's just... you told me you had a gynecologist appointment today that you couldn't reschedule." The corner of my mouth lifted.

As shitty as the past ten minutes had been, there was one bright, shining moment I would savor. I caught my boss in a lie.

She endlessly reminded us at work how honesty was important. That if we ever lied to her about missing work, we would be fired on the spot, no questions asked.

My heart jumped in my chest. Would she fire herself? God, I hoped so.

Her lips pursed. She knew I had her. After an achingly uncomfortable moment where her gaze bounced around the room, she said, "I had that appointment—"

"You did? That's strange because I didn't meet you at a doctor's office—"

"As I was saying," she cut Andrew off, speaking loudly over him, "I had the appointment, but it didn't take very long. And after, I came here—"

"To fuck my boyfriend." I folded my arms and glared.

I'd been working damn hard to become a veterinarian for the past three years. I was elated when I graduated with my veterinarian degree and got a job at the only veterinarian clinic in a twenty-five-mile radius of this tiny town, Castle Ridge. I started as an animal tech, but Angelica promised she'd promote me once I took the tests and became a certified veterinarian. I took the tests and became certified right away.

That was a year and a half ago, and here I was, still a tech.

Any other person would have quit. Not only did she lie about the promotion, but she had been banging my boyfriend in my bed.

But I couldn't leave the veterinarian clinic. Why? Because I loved the animals too damn much.

Since I didn't own a car, there would be no way I could get a job with another veterinarian some-where else. Working with animals was my passion, and I wouldn't let these bozos take that away from me.

I sighed.

"Daisy? Daisy? You zoned out there for a moment. Are you okay? You're not having a stroke, are you?"

"No, I'm not having a damn stroke. Trust me, even my blood vessels know you're not worth clogging up over." My nose flared as I inhaled. "You know what...? You're right. I do need to leave."

I stomped toward the closet to grab some of my things. "And when I walked home from work today, I actually felt bad about not being there for you. I felt *guilty* because I had been so busy with work."

My eyes slid to my boss, who yawned once more, and the sheets slipped. One of her nipples peeped out, and it kind of pissed me off. Her boob looked perfect.

I easily lost a guy to a woman who was not only more attractive than me, but more successful too. If those were the rules for relationships, I would never win.

I focused on the clothes and not the idiots in my bed. "I felt bad because I've been working so much and volunteering at the animal shelter. Being so tired, and I haven't been there for you. So I bought Chinese at your favorite restaurant and brought it home, thinking we could have a pleasant night in...

maybe get a little romantic. Obviously, I am too late for that."

My boyfriend snorted.

I meant ex-boyfriend, because as of ten minutes ago, I hoped to never see him again.

"Don't worry, Andrew. I'll leave and let you two snuggle for the evening."

My ex smiled at me. "Thanks, Daisy. I'm gonna be real honest here. I thought you would be happy about this. Relieved that we wouldn't have to have sex anymore." Then I heard him mumble, "I know I am."

I took off my food-covered shoes and socks and seriously thought about throwing them at him. But knowing him, he wouldn't clean up the mess, and I didn't want to ruin the sheets as I planned to keep them.

Instead, I took my socks and shoes off and turned to face him. "You thought I would be happy you're sleeping with my boss behind my back? Am I only a motherly roommate to you? Because the way I look at it, that was our relationship the past year. I take care of the home, and you act like a spoiled little baby who can't be bothered to do anything while I work and pay the bills."

Then I turned to face Angelica with a wide smile. "Good luck. Now you get to take care of him all by yourself."

He winced while her green eyes widened in surprise. I bet she never considered what the outcome of all the sex would be.

"You play stupid games, you win stupid prizes." I stared at her as I waved my hand at her prize, Andrew.

"Not really sneaking behind your back when I was planning on telling you. I thought it would be a tremendous weight off your shoulder to know that I'm getting satisfied outside of our relationship, and you won't have to worry about that anymore."

My heart sank to my stomach, and I wondered if I was about to throw up. My mouth fell open at his utter coldness.

My boss added her two cents, which nobody asked for, "I agree, Daisy. Maybe you two shouldn't break up. You can support him, and I can satisfy him. You be the mother while I be the lover."

Wow.

"Apparently, we're all a bunch of fucking robots. Literally. Fucking. Robots. We screw each other and have no emotions," I yelled as I waved my arms in the air.

I was angry and sick of trying to make sense of the two other people in the bedroom. It was time to go.

Andrew shook his head at my rant while my boss rubbed her chin.

Watching the both of them, I realized something. Whatever Andrew thought was going on between them, it was obviously not going to last. I knew enough about people to realize he not only screwed me over, but also himself.

"I'm not a robot." I pressed my hand to my chest. "I have feelings for you. Excuse me, let me correct myself. I *had* feelings for you."

I took a breath to gather myself before I exploded with robot nonsense again. "I'm going to leave. I vehemently hope there's some good fortune coming my way, and I never have to see you again, Andrew. Just let me grab a few more things."

Angelica sighed.

"So incredibly sorry if it inconveniences you." I mock-frowned at my boss as I rolled my eyes.

"Oh, no trouble. But you should really think about it, Daisy. We could still live together and be there for each other," Andrew said, totally oblivious to my sarcasm.

He kept going, but I focused on packing a bag to get out. "Like you mentioned, we could eat Chinese food together and do other couple stuff. But I would only have sex with Angelica. Just think about it." He winked.

I shuddered. He was repulsive.

Slipping on some new socks and shoes, I grabbed the bag I had been packing. "That's it. Now you can go back to your banging with a clear conscience. Don't need to worry about the girlfriend walking in on you."

"I'm glad there are no hard feelings, Daisy." Andrew got up but realized he was still naked, so he quickly moved back under the white sheets.

I held up my middle finger to show him how hard my feelings really were before I walked out.

"See you on Monday," Angelica called out once I left the room.

My shoulders slumped. "Yup. See you Monday."

Because she was right. A stark reminder that she was the only vet in town.

My life was crap.

Making it to the front door as the tears pricked the back of my eyes, I picked up the keys I had tossed just twenty minutes ago. I shoved them into the front pocket of my pants and walked out the door.

My stomach grumbled, reminding me that even my dinner was ruined tonight.

Even if I had to work with Angelica, I hoped I never saw Andrew's slimy face ever again.

2

CILLIAN

"You're telling me that my own teammates call me Grumpy Old Man? I'm only thirty-two years old," I said as I turned the steering wheel to take a left on Fitzlee Street.

I watched my coach rub the front of his face as he sighed. "Look, Cillian... they say it with affection."

I rolled my eyes. "If that's affection, I'd love to see their idea of irritation." Then I mumbled under my breath, "Maybe then they'd take the game a little more seriously."

I thought my coach farted. Turned out it was only him turning in the car's leather seat to glare at me. I knew why he wouldn't take his eyes off me—my attitude around other people irritated him.

Yes, I was rough around the edges, but that was only because my teammates needed to work harder. I had to be there for them, show them what needed to get done. Sometimes, I had to yell it to their face until they understood.

I was a hockey player on the Blue Ridge Mountain Devils. We're a national hockey team, but we weren't high in the ranks—which was exactly why we all needed to take the game more seriously.

They goofed around more than was necessary. "Coach, I know you mean well. You're saying this to me to help me out. But what if something big happened? What if we got a chance at the Cup? Would they even know what to do?"

"Jeez, Cillian, you act like they're a bunch of bumbling fools. They wouldn't be on the team if they weren't the best."

I shrugged as I turned on his street. The streetlamp above highlighted the sprinkling of rain.

"You're right. It's just... ugh, I'm going to try." I shook my head. "Try to be more positive."

There was silence. I thought Coach would be happy I was admitting I was wrong. I didn't do that too often.

Glancing over at him as I pulled up to his house, I saw he was rubbing his thumb over his knuckle. He only did that when he had something difficult to say, like when he told me about my mom.

"Cillian, I think you know you're getting up there in age, right?"

"You think I'm too old for this?" My heart thundered in my chest. "I've known players nearing forty. and they're still playing great hockey."

The world outside was disappearing as the windows fogged.

"That's not what I meant. It's just, you know..." He glanced around as if he suddenly realized we stopped. "Oh, look, I'm home. Well, I will see you on Monday—"

"No, no, don't do that." I reached over to grab his shoulder to stop him from hopping out of my Lexus SUV. "I know we're at your house, but I want to talk about this more. You aren't planning on letting me go, are you?"

That would be my worst nightmare. I had wanted to be a hockey player since I was five years old and my dad bought me a hockey stick for my birthday. The feeling of hitting a puck and watching it fly away at lightning speed was indescribable.

I knew I had to retire one day. I just thought it would be on my terms, not getting kicked off a team for being a grouch.

God, was I that bad?

Coach's lips thinned as he smiled. "How about Monday? We'll have a discussion and talk more about it then. Enjoy the weekend. Relax. Maybe hang out with the guys from the team. If you don't like the little nickname they gave you, then make them change their minds."

I tilted my head. "You want me to yell at them until they change it?"

"No. God, why does it always go there with you? No yelling or fighting. Just be nice and friendly with them. That's all."

I was listening to him and not liking what he was saying, but he was the coach. I wasn't good at being nice. Now that I thought about it, I wondered when I smiled last?

Coach used to play hockey when he was younger. He knew the power of teamwork, so I nodded. "I know you're right."

His brow rose. "Oh, really?"

"I'll think about it. And I'll definitely relax this weekend. Maybe I'll call Emmanuel, and we'll hang out. Get some pizza and watch a game."

"Yeah, Cillian, sit at home and watch a game. Like you do every night," Coach mumbled as he turned to open the door.

"What? It sounded like you said, you do every night."

"Never mind, Cillian, just enjoy your weekend and be back for practice on Monday. We've got a game next week."

I waved. "Okay, Coach, you have a good night." I watched him walk up to his house. His young kid opened the door to greet him, and then his wife appeared and leaned over, giving him a kiss on his cheek. And when they turned back, they saw me staring.

Instead of waving, I straightened in my seat and pulled away. Was it creepy for me to watch them? To be jealous of what coach had? Possibly.

I was hungry, and there was only one place to go when hunger struck. *Pizza Joe's.*

Checking the time, I hoped I'd get the order in before they closed. I tapped the smart screen in the car and instantly called up my favorite pizza joint. It didn't take long to order because Joe had it memorized.

Once the call was done, I thought about what Coach said to me. It had been a rough day on the ice, and maybe I had been a little too hard on some of the guys.

I should be nicer to them. Yell less. Perhaps even give out a compliment or two. I sucked in a breath. That wouldn't be easy. The last time I gave compliments was two years ago.

A surprising image popped into my head. Images of the coach's wife kissing him on the cheek. My fingers gripped the steering wheel tighter.

I didn't have a thing for his wife. It was what they had together that sent a sharp pain through my heart.

How could I be nice to people when it only brought heartache?

I hadn't always been the grumpy hockey player, but I learned the hard way why it didn't pay to be sweet. When you're kind to people, they use you and take advantage of your kindness. The more I thought about Coach and his loving family, the angrier I became. Not at him or his family, of course, but at life. I knew firsthand that kindness never got you love.

But for hockey, I could be nicer. Our team was good, not the best, but good. Maybe if I tried it Coach's way, we could be the best.

I turned into the strip mall parking lot. It was late on a Friday, so there were no other cars. I pulled up and parked. Sitting there, I looked at the red and blue neon sign for Pizza Joe's.

Every so often, it flickered. The only shop filled with light was the pizza place. I knew I was cutting it close with my order, but Joe liked me—mainly because I ordered so much pizza.

I knew many people like tacos, and I understood that. Call me old-fashioned, but I was a pizza guy. And Pizza Joe's had the best pizza in Castle Ridge or just about anywhere.

I had been to New York many times and had eaten their pizza. And yeah, it was excellent, but nothing beat Pizza Joe's.

My stomach growled, and I shook off that jealousy for love. I wanted to enjoy my night. A great night of sitting at home with my dad watching an old hockey game.

Hopefully, I'd learn something new from those old players. I always tried to improve my game.

All while enjoying my favorite food with the best dad anyone could ask for. Besides, it brought a little enjoyment to my dad's life. He loved pizza and hockey too. Guess it was in our genes.

My dad deserved that happiness. He was all I had, and I was all he had since Mom passed.

I sighed but hopped out of the car. Enough with the memories... They only brought pain.

Once I opened the glass door to the pizza joint, it surprised me to see somebody in there, considering it was closing time. When I talked to Joe, he told me I added the last order of the night. I guess she ordered right before me.

There was something familiar about the young woman standing at the tall counter. Her long brown hair glistened in the fluorescent lighting.

I glanced up at the menu overhead, not that I was going to order anything else, just habit.

"Be right with you," Joe's deep voice came from the back.

When I turned to the woman, it hit me how I knew her—she was Jackson's little sister. "Hello, Daisy," I said with a frown.

My teammate Jackson was a little cocky shit everyone loved. Everyone but me.

And he hated me. I never understood what went up his ass and died.

Staring at Daisy, I made the mistake of settling on her beautiful large brown eyes that I swore bore deep into my soul. They took my breath away.

One night many years ago, I took a chance with her and instantly regretted it. She wanted nothing to do with me.

"Cillian." She frowned because, obviously she would.

Nobody seemed to like me, maybe because I was too grumpy, like Coach said. But I had dealt with people who had attitudes before, and I didn't out-right hate them. They could have had a bad day. You never knew.

"So, what brings you here tonight?" I asked to be polite.

While she wasn't a teammate, I thought I could practice my niceness skills on her. But what did it matter? She probably didn't even want to talk to me.

She groaned.

I knew it.

"Just trying to get food, and since every store and restaurant around here closes when the sun goes down, I thought pizza. Pizza Joe's is open late."

I nodded and was about to add something, but she had an urgent need to keep speaking.

"I'm hungry, and apparently, we are all robots. As a robot, I need fuel. And after spilling Chinese food all over myself, I can't get fuel that way, so it's pizza."

My head jerked back. She wasn't reacting well to my kindness. I glanced around to find my reflection in the large metal pizza behind the counter. Did I look strange smiling? Was that why she was talking about robots?

"Spilling Chinese food on yourself sounds bad. Clumsy, huh?" I just went with it.

"Yes. Clumsy. I'm so clumsy." Her arms rose into the air.

Apparently, the nice thing I was trying wasn't working. Kindness wasn't in my genes. Like, the nicer I became, the crazier people were around me.

"Hey, Cillian. I just finished your order." Joe waddled out with a large pizza box in his hand. He had a thick head of black hair that was always plastered back with pomade. I knew it was pomade because my dad used the same type. I could smell it the moment I walked into his restaurant—it even overpowered the pizza scent.

"I'm sorry, miss, but this is his order. I can't let you have it."

"But I'm willing to pay double. I really am hungry, and I've had the worst day on earth."

My eyes slid over to Daisy.

Fuck being nice.

"The worst, you say?"

"Yeah, the worst." She emphasized it by groaning, her head falling back.

"I've had the worst day before. But never thought of stealing somebody else's pizza from them."

She shook her head and placed her hand on my arm. My eyes zeroed in on her touch. Normally I'd tell her to get her hands off me, but something happened. There was a tingle where her hand rested on my arm—a nice tingle.

"Cillian, I know this is your pizza, but please have a heart. All the places are closed, and I only want some food. I'll pay you." She smiled, but I noticed the redness around her eyes.

She wasn't lying when she said she had a bad day. I could tell, but no one came between me and my pizza—not even a distressed but pretty young woman.

19

My heart broke for her, though it only lasted one second.

Her smile hardened, and I knew that look. My ex-girlfriend gave me that expression once. She pretended she cared when, in actuality, her heart was made of ice.

So, no, this was my pizza.

I reached over and took the pizza from Joe. He nodded, knowing I had already paid using his app.

"I'm going home. I'm hungry too. And you aren't the only one who has hard days. There's an entire world of people who had harder days than you. Should I give them a pizza too?"

She shook her head as she gazed at the gray-tiled floor. "No. I didn't mean—"

"Nobody ever means anything, but maybe they should. Maybe they should just say the truth instead of sucking up to get what they want."

I knew that was uncalled for, but I was in a bad mood. So much for trying to be nice.

Maybe I could try again when I wasn't hungry and tired and dealing with a woman who didn't know the first thing about bad days.

I slammed a twenty on the counter and walked out the door. Joe deserved a big tip.

Her problems were not my problems.

Anyone else who didn't like me because they were having a bad day? Well, then that was their problem and not mine.

3

DAISY

"What happened to you? Did you catch Andrew in bed with another woman?" My brother's smile widened with pride at his on-the-nose tragic joke.

I stood on his front doorstep as the icy rain soaked through my sweater until it burned my skin. "Funny, coming from a man with a black eye." I waved for him to let me inside.

Some people thought it was amusing that my brother didn't comprehend basic etiquette, like not letting a person get rained on while standing at his front door by inviting them inside. I never saw the humor in it.

He flashed me a stunned expression and then nodded, stepping aside. "Where's your coat?"

"Forgot it." I slugged the large plastic bag from my shoulder and let it land with a sloppy thud on the square tiles in his front entrance.

He laughed. "You forgot it? That sounds like something I would do. It's pouring rain out, Daisy."

I threw my head back and laughed, because why not? At least I wasn't crying… anymore. I had been sobbing the whole walk over. Loud, overly dramatic weeping that I hadn't done since I was fifteen years old. And that was only when our elderly dog, Bensen, got hit by a car.

My brother didn't need to know about my ridiculous tears. Thankfully, the rain covered up the trails they left behind.

Just before I reached my brother's door, I decided I was tired of wasting my emotions on a man who thought cheating on his girlfriend was the equivalent of helping pay a bill, like it was a good thing. I felt numb at his sheer stupidity and my ineptitude at not realizing I was wasting years of my life with a moron.

"It seems you're right, Jackson."

"Right about what?" His brow crinkled.

I turned to face him and stared as my brother's face morphed from confusion into concern. I felt the tears brew behind my eyes but shook them off.

No. No more tears.

"I walked in on Andrew in bed with another woman… the other woman being my boss."

His smile faded. "What? Oh, Daisy, I'm so sorry. Oh, my god. I feel like an idiot."

I loved my brother with all my heart, but he was an idiot. I was born with the brains, and he was born with the brawn, hence why he was a hockey player.

But, still, he meant well.

"It's not your fault, Jackson. I'm sure you were only joking about Andrew cheating."

His brown eyes slid to the side as he mumbled, "Yeah, I was joking."

"What?"

He waved his hand in the air. "Nothing, Daisy. I'm so sorry. You're soaked. Let me go get you a towel." He headed down the hallway of his miniscule one-bedroom apartment. "Make yourself comfortable on the couch. I'll see if I have anything you can wear. I'll be right back."

The floor creaked despite it being heavily carpeted. He used to have a big house when he was with his wife, but when they divorced—which was her idea—she took him for everything.

I knew what Katie was the moment I met her, and that was a gold digger. There wasn't much of a way to make money in a small town up in the Blue Ridge Mountains of Virginia. Unless you became a social media personality, which she tried, but the woman was not good at much in life, and that included getting followers on her VidTube account.

The only thing she did was help create my nephew, Lucas. He was the only reason I tolerated her.

But being a mom was too much for her, so she left when he was only one. They divorced when he was two, and now she only saw him about once a month.

Despite all that, my brother still loved her. She took all his money, left him to raise their son all on his own, and only came back when she wanted something. Yet he hoped they'd get back together one day.

Jackson was the nicest guy and would do anything for the people he loved, and Katie took advantage of that. Our father raised us to treat people with respect, but I couldn't respect her.

"Okay, here we go. Got a towel." He held a small hand towel up victoriously.

I shook my head but grabbed it, wiping down my face.

"Lucas is coming. He wants to show you a book he got." My brother tried to smile, but it didn't reach his eyes.

He loved his son with every cell of his heart, but he hoped Lucas would fall in love with sports like he had when he was young. Unfortunately, his four-year-old only seemed to be interested in books. That was where I took over.

Since his mother and father split, I became a motherly figure to my nephew. While I had a passion for helping animals, I also loved books.

"Oh no. I didn't wake him, did I?"

Jackson shook his head. "Nah, I caught him reading under his window. He was using the light from the outside streetlamp to read."

Smart kid. I rolled my lips over my teeth, trying not to giggle. "That's terrible."

My brother's eyes narrowed. "Don't pretend like you didn't enable him with those books you always show up with. And then story time over at the Castle

Ridge Library." He snorted and crossed his arms over his chest. "You know what you are, Daisy…? You're a book pimp."

I pushed my hands onto my damp jean-clad hips and took a step closer to my brother. "Take that back. I'm only sharing my love of books with my nephew. You're just jealous because he loves books more than hockey."

Jackson's nose flared. I had crossed the line. The moment the words exited my mouth, I knew I had gone too far.

"I didn't mean that, Jackson. I'm sorry—"

He held up his hand. "No, you're right. I don't understand. What kid doesn't love to hit a ball with a stick? I'd even be happy if he liked… you know, those non-athletic sports, like golf. Hell, at this point I'd even settle for chess."

"He's four," I said, though I knew my brother wasn't listening anymore.

It's not that he hated his son reading—he didn't mind it at all—and he knew it would be helpful for him when he started school next year. It was Lucas's obsession with books, combined with his total disinterest in sports, that upset Jackson. His son had become the total opposite of him, and he couldn't relate.

My brother rubbed his brow and was about to continue his tirade when a miniature version of him came bounding down the creaking hallway. "Hi, Auntie Daisy. What book did you bring me?"

My brother pointed his finger at me. "Book pimp."

I frowned. Maybe I had been spoiling him with a lot of books. I realized I always brought a book—or two or five—every time I came over.

Bending down until I sat on my haunches, I smiled at the little boy who stole my heart the moment I held him in the hospital. His mother refused to take her eyes off me until I returned him. Katie never liked me, and the feeling was totally mutual.

"I'm sorry, Lucas. I worked late today and didn't have time to get any at the library for you. How about we go tomorrow, and you can pick them out yourself?"

That got a smile from him. My heart melted as the dimples appeared on his cheeks. He was so darn cute.

"Yes, I'd like that. But, Auntie Daisy, why are you all wet? Didn't Daddy tell you that if you stand out in the rain, you'll catch a cold?"

My eyes shifted up to my brother. "No. Your daddy didn't tell me that. I think a good idea for books we can check out tomorrow would be about the weather. Would you like to learn about the weather and where rain comes from?"

His blue eyes lit up. "Oh, yes. That would be great."

I mussed up his mop of brown hair, and Lucas pushed my hand away. He hated when I did that, but his hair was so soft. I only did it to prevent myself from wrapping my soggy arms around him for a hug. The boy was so huggable.

My brother cleared his throat. "Hey, Auntie Daisy?" Jackson lifted his brows. "It's a little late, and we should get back to bed."

I looked at my wrist as if I had a watch... which I didn't.

"Oh, yeah, it is late, isn't it?" I gave my brother a wink. "Lucas, how about this? I'm going to get myself dried off, and then I'm going to come in and read you a bedtime story. And after that, you go to sleep. No more reading."

"Yes." He clapped his hands and ran off down the hall. "Auntie Daisy, I'll be waiting in my bedroom for you," he called out as he shuffled into his room.

Which was also my brother's room since the apartment was only a one-bedroom. My brother slept on a full-sized bed that was just wide enough for his frame, but I knew his feet hung off the end.

Little Lucas slept in his adjustable toddler bed. He had inherited my brother's height, so I knew it wouldn't be long before he needed a bigger bed. When that happened, I hoped there would be enough room to walk around in the bedroom for them.

I smiled. "He's the sweetest boy in all the world."

"Yes, he is. He really is." My brother sighed but then turned to face me. "If you need to stay here tonight, I have the couch." He pointed to the voluminous but not very long leather couch in his small living room area. "It doesn't pull out or anything, but it's comfortable."

He meant comfortable for a short person like me. Since he was six-foot-three, the couch wouldn't even fit his legs if he lay on it.

"Actually, I would like to stay here. I don't want to go back to my place... not right now." I shrugged.

"Of course, Daisy, anything you want. When you're ready to go back over there, I'll go with you. I'll be happy to help you get rid of any unwanted pests."

"Jackson, you don't have to do that." I waved my hands at him.

My brother shook his head. "You're too nice, Daisy. That man walked all over you, and you let him. You need to be assertive and take care of you. Even with the animals. You're willing to work at a place where the boss treats you like crap and had the nerve to sleep with your boyfriend. Yet, on Monday, you will walk into that place like nothing happened. Am I right?"

I groaned. My brother knew me too well.

I nodded. "What can I do? I don't own a car, and she's the only vet in town. My career is important to me, just like your career is important to you."

He rubbed his forehead. "You always have choices, Daisy. Like me, for example. I have the choice to listen to you and not make Andrew pay, or I have the choice to beat the crap out of him. I think you know what my choice will be."

4

CILLIAN

It was Saturday night, and I had the perfect evening planned. One with my dad, watching a classic hockey game. What more could a man ask for?

It was so great that I did it every night. When you stumble upon perfection, you recreate it any chance you got.

There was a knock at the door just as I was settling into my recliner. And little did I know, the entire night would be ruined by what awaited on the other side of that door.

I opened it, discovering my good friend and teammate, Emmanuel, standing there. His dark curls were tousled and wet, but a big grin was on his face.

Typical for Emmanuel. Nothing ever got him down, not even a cold, rainy night.

"Hey, Cillian. I've come to collect you to take you to the big party tonight."

I groaned like I usually did whenever people asked me to take part in things. Except for hockey. That was the only thing I loved to do. It was my job, after all. I was lucky in life, getting to do what I loved for a living.

"I already have plans. I'm staying in and hanging out with my dad."

A wave of laughter burst out of Emmanuel's mouth, and his head fell back. I thought he might drown from the amount of raindrops that fell in as he choked out his chuckles. I stood there and stared at him, unaware of what was so amusing.

After a few seconds, he lifted his head, his smile and laughter fading away. "Oh, you're serious. What are you, eighty?"

"I'm thirty-two," I said as he stared at me, unconvinced. "Emmanuel, it's really nice that you were thinking of me and came all the way over here to take me to a party. But as you can tell, it's freezing and rainy outside, and it's warm in here. I have pizza on the way. I'm watching a classic hockey game with my dad, so the last thing I want to do is go to a party where everyone hates me."

I knew what he was about to say as his mouth opened, and I held up my hand. "Yes, I know how disliked I am on the Devils. I can't help it if I take hockey seriously." I shrugged. "I guess people would rather I loosen up and be more carefree, but that's not who I am."

Emmanuel blinked, unable to argue with my logic.

It was important to me to make my dad proud. Perhaps even be team captain one day. I liked Brian, our current team captain, and I knew it would be a long time before he retired. He was only two years older than me. In the meantime, I wanted to stay focused and be the best player so my teammates would elect me one day for captain.

It would make my dad proud if he saw me as captain. Perhaps I'd get to witness that spark in his eyes one more time—the same spark that died out two years ago.

"Wow, dude, seriously? You sound so old right now. Come on, who cares if it's cold and raining? There's this thing that's been invented... maybe you heard of it. *Umbrellas.* I've got umbrellas. I'm sure you have an umbrella—"

"I don't have an umbrella," I lied.

I figured not letting him in the house and the continual rain pelting his head would cause him to change his mind about convincing me to go to the party, but it didn't.

"Okay, well, it's not that far. I got a car." He waved out into the darkness behind him, where I was sure his car was parked. "We're going to be in the car the whole time going to the party. My car has heat. The party has heat."

He made a face as if he was unsure the party was actually heated.

"Look, Emmanuel, I understand you want me to come, but I'm still gonna say no. I promised my dad I'd stay here, and we'd have a guy's night in."

As I was about to close the front door, my father yelled out from the living room, "Son, you need to go."

My eyes widened as I turned and glanced back into the living room. My dad sat there in his own brown leather recliner, holding a beer can in his hand, gazing right back at me.

"I'm sorry, Son, but you are young. And those are your teammates. You should be with them. Not with an old man like me."

"Dad, you're only sixty-two. You're not that old."

"I'm old enough to know that when there's a party and your teammates are involved, you should go and hang out with them. Don't use rain as an excuse to have pizza and watch a game you already know the outcome of with your father. We do that every night, anyway. Do something different for once."

I was about to respond when my dad pointed at me. "And not *The Golden Girls*. God help me, I'm sick of that joke. I think I'll be scarred for life."

I smirked at his hatred of the old 80s television show.

"You do this every night? Oh, man... that's just sad." Emmanuel shook his head.

My lips thinned. Emmanuel pushed past me, inviting himself inside.

"Hey," I said as he knocked me out of the way.

He stepped into the hallway and shook himself like a dog drying off, covering the hardwood floor in droplets. As I thought about it, he was kind of like those dogs everyone loved. Emmanuel was the Labrador Retriever of hockey players.

It was as if my dog, Arizona, could sense I was thinking about another animal because he yelped and trotted his way over to me, curling at my feet. He, too, was a Labrador, but unusually small, half the size of a regular adult Lab.

Five years ago, my parents took a trip to Arizona and saw an animal rescue from the café where they were having lunch. My mother insisted they just look. My father always rolled his eyes whenever he told the story. He knew they would end up adopting a dog that day because my mom had an enormous heart. She always had to help anyone who needed it. That was why she became a nurse.

Until she was the person who needed the help...

Arizona and my mom were inseparable. And when she passed, it was as if something died in both my dad and Arizona.

I took over caring for him. My father still walked the dog, but sometimes it was as if he'd look at Arizona and only see my mom's heart. That was when I had to watch the dog. My dad would usually stay the rest of the day in his bedroom.

I lived with him because there was no way I was leaving my dad alone with his thoughts. My teammates might have laughed at me for staying in with my dad every night, but he needed me.

"I agree with your father. He makes sense. Are you sure you two are related?" Emmanuel joked as he walked over to my dad and introduced himself.

I watched them make small talk and groaned, then shut the front door. I had a feeling I was going to go to a party tonight, whether I wanted to or not. Especially since I now had two men ganging up on me.

I looked down at Arizona and scooped him up in my arms. "You want me to stay, don't you, Arizona?"

My dog squirmed in my arms and yelped, insisting I put him back down. I had my answer. Three males were now against me.

"Emmanuel, I know you mean well, but honestly, I really want to stay in tonight. You know, get some rest so I'll be ready for practice on Monday."

"Do you even know who the party is for, Cillian?"

I shook my head. "Of course I don't. Why would I know anything about a party I don't want to attend?"

Emmanuel sat on the couch in between the two recliners. The dark brown leather creaked as he eased back.

The corner of my teammate's lips curled as he said, "It's for Daisy Haynes. You know, Jackson's little sister? It's her twenty-fifth birthday party. A lot of guys from the team are going to be there to help her celebrate."

I stopped listening after he uttered Daisy's name. I rubbed my face. After the way I treated her at Pizza Joe's, I was sure she wouldn't want me at her party.

She was a beautiful young woman, and I was just some hardened hockey player who would rather stay home on a Saturday night and watch an old game with his old man.

I regretted what I said to her. I could have at least given her a slice or two of the pizza. The woman deserved better, and I knew it.

Too many memories had popped into my head that night. Then, when Daisy appeared at *Pizza Joe's*, the memory of the kiss we shared—the kiss she instantly regretted—came bubbling to the surface.

I remembered her frown too clearly... and the puke that came after. Yes, apparently, I caused women to puke when I kissed them.

It was time for her to stop taking up space in my head. I tried to focus on hockey. Anything, really, so I didn't think about her, or her lips.

"If it's her birthday, I'm pretty sure she doesn't want me there."

"Son, stop making excuses."

"I'm not making excuses, Dad," I said through gnashed teeth. "I want to stay in tonight. Don't make me bring up the farm."

Of course I was making up an excuse. Discovering Daisy would be there only made me want to stay home that much more.

My dad was one to talk. All he did now was make excuses why he couldn't go out. Even to places close by, like the grocery store. But the worst was why he wouldn't go back to the home he raised me in, the farm.

I knew he had aches and pain sometimes, but that wasn't the reason he refused to leave the house. He should be out, especially since he didn't want to work on the farm anymore. But discussing the farm with my dad was a touchy subject. I couldn't talk to him about anything that reminded him of Mom.

Even with all that love in my heart for the man who helped raise me, it didn't mean I wasn't a little pissed at him right now. Because I wanted to stay home too.

I opened my mouth, about to apologize to my dad, when there was a knock at the door.

"What now?" I grumbled.

Was someone else from the team trying to beg me to go to the party? I opened the door, and the scent of warm, gooey pepperoni pizza hit my nostrils before I noticed the wet pizza delivery guy standing in front of me. Water dripped off his trucker hat with the pizzeria logo, onto the black insulator bag protecting my delicious pizza.

My stomach grumbled.

I quickly gave him the money I owed and a tip before he slid the cardboard pizza box out and handed it over. The way my stomach was acting, I wouldn't have been surprised if I woke up tomorrow officially married to a pizza box.

Thanking him, I shut the door and held out the box of the most perfect food combination to ever exist.

I glanced over to the couch and noticed fear in Emmanuel's dark brown eyes. He knew my feelings about pizza and realized he would not be getting me out that door tonight.

"You know there's gonna be food at the party. I think one of Daisy friend's is a chef. So... definitely amazing food."

I just gazed at the pizza, completely ignoring Emmanuel, and made my way into the kitchen, where I placed the box on the marble counter. Footsteps came up behind me.

"Please come, Cillian."

I kept my back to Emmanuel. "No."

"A lot of guys from the team will be there. They'd love to see you."

"I doubt that." I opened the box and inhaled, ignoring both my teammate and the words my coach said yesterday, which were still floating in my head.

God, I love pizza.

"Despite what you think, the team doesn't hate you. They just think you take things too seriously sometimes. If you show up at the party, they might start thinking you're not as uptight as they thought."

I pressed my hands against the counter, then pushed away, turning to face him. "Emmanuel, most people are selfish assholes." His eyes widened, but I continued, "Arizona isn't a selfish asshole. Well, most of the time he isn't." I waved at my dog, who was sniffing the air slowly, making his way into the kitchen. "Animals aren't like that. I'd rather hang out with my dog or watch a game with my dad than socialize with a bunch of drunk people on a Saturday night. You know what's going to happen if I go?"

Emmanuel slowly shook his head.

"Someone is going to spill their drink on me. Another person will say something totally inappropriate to one woman there, and I'll be the only sober one who will make sure the woman is okay. Someone else will break something expensive, and he'll promise to pay for it, but then turn to us to ask if he can borrow some cash."

Emmanuel's eyes slid to the side, and he mumbled, "Aspen."

He knew who I was talking about. He also knew everything I said was true.

"And when I was young, my parents and I would stay in on Saturday nights and watch hockey or a movie while having pizza. I actually like this shit. Maybe it makes me a loser, but it's what I like."

Emmanuel rubbed his forehead. "I didn't want to have to do this, but Brian is going to be there, and he said he had a big announcement... He wanted me to tell you he also wants to speak with you at the party."

The smell of the pizza faded away, and my stomach tightened. "Do you think he wants to talk about..." I slowly stopped talking as I was too afraid to utter the words.

"Maybe." He shrugged. "He's been talking to the guys up in Boston lately. But, hey, you stay here and have pizza. I know Jackson will be at the party, considering it's his little sister's birthday. Since you two are the same age, if you don't show up, Brian will probably talk to Jackson instead."

If Brian was going to announce what I thought he would announce, I might have a chance at team captain earlier than I had expected.

Fuck. I was going to a party tonight.

5

DAISY

"There's something seriously wrong with wanting to hang out alone in a broom closet during your birthday party," my best friend said, twirling a lock of her wavy red hair as she squeezed herself into the room that held me, a mop, broom, blue plastic bucket filled with various cleaners, and a cat.

I clutched the worn book to my chest as if she was about to yank it away, and flattened myself against the wall. "I'm not alone. Fierce is with me." I reached down and slid my fingers over the top of her calico-covered back.

Lydia's golden eyes grew. "I said you could stay here until you're ready to head back to your apartment. I didn't mean you needed to stay in the broom closet." An adorable line appeared between her brows. "Wait a second... Where did that cat come from? You didn't have it this morning when you came here from your brother's place."

"I called Big Mountain Animal Rescue and told them I couldn't come in today. As you know, I volunteer there on weekends. After last night, I needed a day off. But they had no room for the cat, and she had come from such a terrible place. A hoarder. I couldn't say no to helping this little lady out and giving Fierce a temporary home."

Lydia nodded. "Okay, but you really should have asked first. I talked to the roomies, Sophia and Harper, and asked if they had any animal allergies because I knew you worked for a vet and would likely have fur on your clothes. They said no, but I hadn't asked about a pet. Besides, I would have to check to see if the apartment is pet-friendly."

I rubbed my brow. "What about Melanie and Naomi? Aren't they still living here?"

"Yeah, but Melanie is out with some people from her work, and Naomi is visiting her grandmother, who hasn't been well lately."

I glanced down at Fierce as she swatted a dust ball in the corner. "Maybe Jackson can take her? I'm sure Lucas would love to have a cat for a little while."

The past twenty-four hours had been so crazy. I slept on my brother's couch, and it was almost as bad as walking in on Andrew and Angelica. That couch of his was doing its best to break my back. I called Lydia after breakfast to ask if I could sleep on her couch.

I knew there wouldn't be a spare bedroom for me at her apartment. Five women living in a three-bedroom apartment was crowded, to say the least.

"I'll call the animal rescue in the morning and tell them I can't keep her."

Lydia nibbled her lower lip while she watched Fierce lick her front paw. "No, don't do that." She let out a breath. "Ugh, we'll make it work. It's only temporary, right?"

I nodded.

Lydia wouldn't admit it, but she loved animals as much as I did.

We had been best friends since we were ten years old when she moved to Castle Ridge from New York City. To say it was a culture shock for her would be an understatement. I sat next to her and helped her learn that you didn't need alleyways, subways, and city parks to have fun. There were trails to explore and mountains to climb and caves to run screaming from.

When she went to university out of state, we texted each other every day. I hated not seeing her, and she admitted she missed living in Castle Ridge too much. After a year, she transferred to Green Mountain University two towns over. We both vowed never to be away from each other that long again.

"It was stupid of me to say yes without asking you first. I'm sorry. I'll buy everyone coffee in the morning... the good stuff from Hard Grind."

Her mouth made an "O." I knew coffee was her weakness, and Hard Grind had the best coffee in the world. Not that I had ever really traveled outside of Castle Ridge, but I suspected that its coffee was better than most.

"Yes, the cat can stay. I'll work my magic on the roomies, and you work your magic on the closet." She frowned. "You don't have to stay in the closet... but I do have a blow-up mattress that would fit this space perfectly."

There was something comforting about the tiny room.

"I'm kind of limited in my options since I make little where I work, and I'm already paying for an apartment I'm not living in."

Her brows rose. "You mean you aren't planning on quitting?"

"I'm worried about the animals. Angelica isn't that good of a vet, and I'm not saying that because I hate her. I'm saying that because our front desk assistant, Diana, gets calls from pet owners daily, complaining about Angelica's attitude and how she doesn't listen to what the owner has to say about their pet. You don't even want to know how many times I've saved a pet from her death claws."

She shook her head but had a small grin. "You and animals... I totally picture you living on a farm one day. Some animal sanctuary where you commune with them every day, and where every single one of them is a rescue."

I smirked. "That sounds kind of amazing. I'll be the crazy cat lady, but intensified. The crazy animal lady. Because there's no way I'm ever dating a guy as long as I live. I'll have the animals to make me happy."

"Oh my god, please tell me you're not talking about—"

"What? No. That's where your mind went when I said that? I care for animals; I'm not *attracted* to them." I pretended to puke.

"Sorry, a little tipsy." She giggled. "Enough talk about animals and terrible bosses. Let's head out of this closet for fun. It's your birthday, the big two-five. There are hot guys out there. Jackson invited the hockey team, and they showed up looking super-hot!"

Memories of trying to snag a slice of pizza from a hockey player Friday night surfaced in my head. "Everyone on the team?" I asked.

"Not everyone, but a lot."

"Cillian? Did he show?" I hated even asking, but I didn't want any reminders of Friday.

"Cillian?" She tapped her chin. "Who is Cillian? I get some of them confused. They all look so good without their shirts on. Who can tell them apart?"

I scrunched up my face and folded my arms. "You know Cillian."

"Oh, yeah, the grumpy one." She snorted and shook her head. "I haven't seen him. I don't think he's here."

I felt relief but also a bit sad. I knew why Cillian hated me, but I would have thought he'd let it go by now. One little kiss with puke and a guy never lets you forget.

My cheeks felt warm at the memory. I drank a lot that night, but not too much. I didn't remember kissing the guy I had a crush on since I was eighteen.

Despite how much he hated me, it was still hard to look at him without my stomach doing the excited shuffle. My body might be attracted to him, but his attitude toward me the past few years turned off my crush mode whenever I was around him.

I was wondering if I wasn't meant to date guys, ever.

"Can I sit in here for a while? Enjoy the solitude and maybe read your book."

Lydia sighed. "Okay, but know that both Sophia and Harper have been asking about you. You know Harper likes to make sure everyone is happy and entertained. She might bust in here and grab you."

I nodded. "Tell her I need a minute."

Lydia nodded before leaving, closing the closet door behind her. I leaned back against the wall, knocking over the broom.

"Fierce, never fall for a male cat's charms. He'll be scoping out all the single female cats on the block."

She meowed, and I swear she winked at me. Fierce understood.

"Dear God, it's worse than I thought. You're having conversations with a cat in a broom closet." Harper stood there, flicking her long blond hair off her shoulder.

"It's my birthday. I can do what I want."

"Like live in a closet?"

"It's not like you have an extra bedroom."

"You got me there." Harper stepped into the closet and shut the door.

"It has charm, doesn't it?" I waved around the tiny space as Fierce walked in between her legs.

She narrowed her eyes but surrendered to Fierce's magic as she bent over to pet the purring feline. "Not really. I guess it's a cute idea, Daisy, but maybe another time. We have guests. There's an amazing party going on right outside that door. Hot, muscular men, eager to let loose, are mingling in our living room and kitchen, and if you are feeling up to it, this closet. Or should I say, your bedroom?" She gave me her over-the-top wink as she lifted Fierce and cradled her in her arms.

I nibbled on the bottom of my lip and squeezed the Jane Austen book even tighter. "I'm tired, and I had a long weekend."

"It's only Saturday night."

"*Sense and Sensibility* is all I need to enjoy the night."

Placing the cat back down, Harper shook her head as she plucked the book from my arms and tossed it aside.

"Hey, that's a classic." I glanced back to see where the book landed, but Harper was too quick for me.

She shimmied herself behind me and grab my arms.

"Quick, I got her," she yelled, and a cooling gust of air filled the room as the door swung open.

Sophia stood there. Her thick, lustrous hair the color of silky chocolate cascaded over her shoulders. I had always been jealous of Sophia's hair. We both had brown hair, yet she always looked like she came from a shampoo photoshoot. I told her once she should be a hair model, but she scoffed, telling me she'd never work for The Man.

Harper pushed me forward.

"What are you doi—"

"It's for your own good," Sophia said, stepping aside as Harper pushed me past.

"You're better than this, Daisy. We are doing this out of love," Harper added.

"Lydia said I could stay there—"

"Lydia was the one who told us to do this."

Once Sophia closed the closet and shoved herself against the door so there was no hope of me getting back inside, Harper let me go.

My mouth fell open. I looked around for my best friend, but she was nowhere to be found.

"Having her do your dirty work, I see." I narrowed my eyes at them.

Sophia's lips quirked. "Remember, this is a small town. I wonder what Andrew would say if he found out you were so depressed that you hung out in a closet during your own birthday party."

She didn't play fair. She knew Andrew would love it if I couldn't enjoy a party without him.

I fisted my hands at my side. "Fine. But I'm not eating whatever food you made, no matter how many people rave about it."

Sophia liked to cook when she wasn't working for her dad's car rental business. She dreamed of being a chef one day, and I could totally see that happening. Her food was amazing.

Her emerald eyes flickered to something over my shoulder as she smirked. "Okay. I think there's someone behind you ready to wish you a happy birthday."

Excitement filled my chest as I assumed she meant Jackson was behind me. Maybe he brought Lucas. I'd have a legitimate excuse to hide out in the closet with a book if I was reading to my nephew.

I was so happy that I jumped around, only to discover it wasn't my brother or my nephew. Not only that, but I lost my balance and fell when I landed.

The good news was the guy caught me; the bad news was, it was Cillian, and it wasn't his hands that caught me. It wasn't even his body.

It was his lips.

That's right. I fell onto his mouth for my birthday.

6

CILLIAN

S tuck at a party I didn't want to be at, hunched over in a small closet. Chalk this up to the worst party I had ever been to.

"You don't have to be here. I'm fine," Daisy said as she clutched a book to her chest.

"Really? Tell that to your friends." I threw my thumb over my shoulder.

"You two aren't coming out until you kiss and make up," one of her friends said, followed by laughter.

She frowned with obvious displeasure at being stuck in the tiny space with me. "First you two force me out, and now you lock me back in. Make up your mind," she called out.

Her cheeks were flushed, and as much as I knew I shouldn't be staring, I couldn't take my eyes off Daisy.

"Happy birthday." I turned my attention to the cat, hoping she hadn't noticed me gawking at her.

"Thanks. This wasn't really what you had in mind when you came here tonight, huh?"

I pulled at the collar of my leather jacket. "I didn't want to come tonight. My teammate, Emmanuel, dragged me here. So, I wasn't really expecting much."

Her frown deepened. "Oh. Did you have other plans?" She hugged the book even tighter.

"Just my usual, pizza while I hung out with the best person in the world."

She nodded. "Right. Of course. That sounds a lot better than being stuck in a closet... with me."

A bead of sweat slid down my brow, tickling my cheek. I scratched at the spot, wiping away the moisture, and wondered what she meant by being stuck here with her.

It was as if she thought I didn't want to be around her... which I didn't. But it was because she didn't like me.

"What do you mean, 'with me'?"

She finally let go of the book and tossed it aside. "I'm not naïve, Cillian. I know you hate me." Daisy threw up her arms. "We kissed once, and I almost threw up on you. I get it. I'd probably hate me too. It seems I'm not really attractive to the opposite sex."

That wasn't what I expected at all when I came here tonight.

"You think I hate you? Because you threw up after we kissed?" I sucked in a breath at the realization of what Daisy admitted. "I thought our kiss made you sick."

Her head lifted from staring at the floor, and an adorable grin curled her lips.

"Cillian, you thought the kiss made me sick?" She shook her head. "Oh no. I had been drinking that night… not so much that I don't remember the kiss or wasn't in a proper state to accept a kiss. But I didn't react well to the alcohol because my body has trouble handling it. If I have more than one glass of beer or wine, I usually become sick. What would normally give someone a pleasant buzz can send me over the edge."

She shrugged. "So I just don't do it anymore. If I do, it's the occasional glass of wine or flute of champagne on New Year's Eve, but that's it." Daisy reached up and covered her forehead with her hand. "I was utterly embarrassed after kissing you, so I avoided you for the rest of the night. I'm sorry you thought I hated you."

I couldn't believe I thought Daisy hated me for the past two years, when in actuality, she had become sick from alcohol.

"Hmm. That's funny." I cringed and shook my head. "Not funny that you threw up, but that you don't really drink. I don't drink either. I'm a recovering alcoholic, and I've been sober for almost two years. I actually became sober a few months after that party."

I studied Daisy for her reaction to my confession. She nodded as if I told her it was raining outside—not the usual response I got from people. People usually said something like, "That must be so hard. I could never do that."

Then they'd treat me as if I was a weird alien to be avoided. When the team went out, they never invited me. I understood why they wouldn't want me tagging along to bars, but if they went out to dinner or anything that didn't involve drinking, I never got an invitation.

It didn't take long to learn that if you didn't get drunk with them, you weren't really part of the team.

"That's the reason I didn't want to come tonight. I don't like to go to parties because there's usually alcohol there, and I don't drink."

"I thought when you said you didn't want to come tonight it was because of me. I guess we were both under the wrong impression." She held out her hand. "Hi, I'm Daisy Haynes. This is my birthday party. It's nice to meet you. Fun fact about me: I'm secretly trying to turn my nephew into a book nerd like me."

I watched her hand hover in the air, waiting to be held. To her, it was a funny little way of starting over. She did not know what that hand meant to me.

I swallowed and reached for her, clasping my hand over hers. A warmth bloomed where we touched. I never thought a handshake could cause my chest to ache. "I'm Cillian. I play hockey with your brother."

She held my hand, waiting for me to continue.

"Something no one knows about me... Uh, I can't defend myself against tickling. I am incapable of fighting back."

She smiled, and it was gorgeous. Her firm shake was brief before letting go.

Her head fell back, and she groaned. Once she lifted it back up, Daisy said, "God, my brother. He hates you."

I chuckled as I stretched my fingers, trying to ease the warm sensation left by her. "I'd say he does. Which is weird because we got along for a year when he first came to the team, and then suddenly, he didn't like me." My brow rose. "Did you tell him about our kiss?"

I had wondered if that was the reason. People didn't start hating you out of the blue; there was always something behind it.

"No. God, I was already embarrassed by throwing up right after it. Telling my brother that I not only kissed his teammate, but then puked on his shoes would be the last thing I'd do." She threw her hands in front of her face in humiliation, as if it just happened.

I reached over and tugged her arms down. "Don't worry about it. That was two years ago. A lot has changed since then."

She glanced down at her wrists I hadn't let go of. Daisy pulled her arms away, wrapping them around her stomach.

I shouldn't have held on for so long. Like I said, it was two years ago. She may not hate me, but it wasn't like she was attracted to me anymore.

"About Friday at the pizza shop... I just want to say sorry. I was having a terrible day. My boyfriend cheated on me and I'd just found out." She rubbed her arms as if the thought iced her to the bone.

"What?"

That couldn't be right. Who would be stupid enough to cheat on Daisy? She was smart, captivating, and the most gorgeous woman I had ever met.

She snorted, proving her utter adorableness. "I came home from a long day at work at the veterinarian clinic and walked in on him in bed, naked, with another woman. As you might expect, I didn't react well."

"I don't think anyone would react well to that."

She frowned but shrugged it off. It was obvious she didn't want me to notice the pain in her eyes.

"I went straight to the pizza shop afterward. I'm sorry, I wasn't trying to take your pizza from you. I was just hungry and feeling sorry for myself."

Daisy was having a terrible day, and I was the asshole who brushed her off. Thinking she had no clue what a bad day was. I couldn't have been more wrong.

Daisy was gorgeous, hard-working, and sweet as pie. Speaking of pie, I should have offered her some of mine that night.

"It's me who should apologize. The coach had told me something I didn't want to hear, and I took it out on you. That was wrong. I was in a bad mood."

"When aren't you in a bad mood?" she mumbled.

My eyes widened as her hand flew to her mouth. She shook her head, letting her hand drop. "I don't know why I said that. I didn't mean it—"

"Yes, you did," I said with a sigh.

"No, Cillian, please—"

I held up my hand. "That's what the coach told me. Basically, he said I was a jerk all the time, telling me to lighten up. And I proved him right with how I treated you that night. So, I'm sorry. You wanted something to eat, and I couldn't even share a slice of pizza with you. The team nicknamed me Grumpy Old Man, and I don't blame them."

I leaned back against the wall, kicking a bucket out of the way. The cat yelped and ran behind Daisy. Since she was the nicest person on earth, Daisy reached down to calm the cat.

Why couldn't I be like that? Even in my apology, I freaked out an animal.

She stood and took a step closer to me. As stuffy as the closet was, my skin pricked from the heat of her body with her chest a mere inch from my stomach.

When Daisy lifted her head, her silky brown waves falling down her back, I had to fist my hand to stop from curling my fingers through her hair. The scent of lavender surrounded me, and all I wanted was to wrap my arms around her.

"You aren't a jerk, and they shouldn't call you Grumpy Old Man." Her lips curled into a smile so bright I felt its warmth in my heart.

"I know what I am... but it's kind of you to say that."

A cute little wrinkle appeared between her brows. "I'm not saying it to be kind. I'm saying it because it's the truth."

Her arm lifted, and I watched those fingers of hers as if they were about to save me from drowning. They fluttered in the air, and when they landed, I felt a twitch in my cock.

Daisy rested her hand on my upper arm, her lips parted, and I swore I saw her beautiful brown eyes dip to my mouth.

Perhaps she was hoping for a redo after her confession about our last kiss. I cleared my throat as she licked her lips.

There was no questioning what she wanted, and I'd happily oblige her. I slipped my arms around her waist and pulled her against me.

She gasped. I waited a moment for her to pull away, but she placed her other hand on my arm.

"How's this?" I asked as my heart thundered in my chest.

Did I have it wrong? Was it a mistake to try again?

"It's fine. Just fine." Her voice was breathy with her reply.

There was no mistake. She wanted it too. I bent my head and let my lips drift over hers. We hadn't kissed, not yet, but the whisper-soft touch from our lips was enough to make me groan.

I took in Daisy one last time before I consumed her. Her cheeks flushed, and her eyes set on my mouth. But it was the faint whimpers that escaped her throat that made me wonder if we wouldn't be naked in the closet before long.

My lips were touching hers once again when a sudden gust of cool air filled the room. In a split second, Daisy pushed out of my hold, blinking at the now-open door, and I was bitter at her loss.

A woman stood there. Someone who hadn't locked us in here.

I was about to reach over to close the door and tell her we occupied the room when she spoke.

"Daisy, I'm so sorry Sophia and Harper locked you in here. I just found out."

I glanced at Daisy, ready for her to explain that we needed privacy.

But that wasn't what happened.

"It wasn't very nice of them. They pulled me out and then threw me back in. Tell them to decide." Daisy paused for a moment, tilting her head in my direction but not actually looking up at me. "I'm just glad you showed up when you did," she said right before she walked out the door and back into her party.

Stunned, I waited for her to return. But as the seconds turned into a minute, I realized my mistake.

The last time she abandoned me, alcohol had sickened her.

What was her excuse going to be this time?

7

DAISY

"Coffee. Beautiful black gold that soothed my aching head. That and the gorgeous gooey egg and cheese biscuit sandwich they serve here." Harper held her coffee cup to her nose as if it were healing her headache.

The coffee at Hard Grind was amazing, but I wasn't sure it could cure hangovers.

"Do you think they need a chef here?" Lydia smiled at Sophia before she looked around the cafe.

"I appreciate what you're doing, but think bigger than a small-town coffee shop. Think Michelin-starred restaurant. I'd love to open my own place, maybe start with a food truck and work my way up. Never work for The Man if I can avoid it," Sophia said, sipping her black coffee.

She noticed us staring at her. "Just thinking out loud..."

Sophia was a self-taught, wanna-be chef, and living in a small town didn't present many opportunities for her dream. Also, her father needed her for his car rental business. She loved her father and felt as if following her dream meant she'd be abandoning him.

Lydia shook her head and pushed her fiery red hair from her face. With a cute smile and tip of her paper coffee cup, she said, "Here's to Daisy. Thanks for taking all of us out for breakfast and coffee."

"Hear, hear." Harper lifted her cup while holding her forehead with her other hand.

"I'll always say yes to free food and drink. Thanks, Daisy." Sophia tilted her head toward me.

I stared at her, and so did everyone else at the small wooden table. Her chestnut hair shifted on her shoulders as a cool breeze wafted over the table. Someone had entered the cafe.

After a minute, I waved my hand at Sophia. "But?"

She raised a brow at me. "But what?"

"Come on, Sophia. I've known you since Lydia moved into the apartment with you and the others a year ago. I know there's a 'but' waiting to leave your mouth. What do you have a problem with? Is it Fierce? Because—"

She held up her hand. "It's not the cat. I like cats and find it nice to have the little guy—"

"Girl. Fierce is a female," I corrected her.

"Little girl." She rolled her eyes. "What I'm trying to say is, I don't always take issue with things."

It wasn't that she was the Negative Nelly of the group. Sophia would be there for us every time we needed her. She was loyal to a T. But Sophia grew up way too young. Her father had her working his car rental business since she was five. If something didn't involve hustling or making a buck from it, then in her mind, it wasn't worth trying.

Lydia narrowed her eyes. "So it's okay; the cat is staying with us... rent-free?"

I glared at Lydia. What was she doing?

Sophia snorted. "I will not charge a cat rent; that's ridiculous."

My shoulders sagged. That was close. It wasn't like I had extra cash lying around.

"It's you who needs to pay rent, Daisy," Sophia said before taking a sip of the coffee I just paid for.

"But it's only been one night." My eyes darted to Harper and Lydia, who both had their mouths wide open.

"I know. Don't worry. We won't need the money for two weeks, not until the end of the month."

"Come on, Sophia. Daisy is our friend. It's not like she's moving in with us. She just needs a place to crash for a few days, right?" Harper took her hand from her forehead and waved it at me.

"Yes, I will not sleep in the broom closet forever." Besides, that blow-up mattress was only slightly better than sleeping on the hardwood floor. I had aches in places in my back I didn't even know had muscles.

"Okay. I thought Andrew had the apartment." She shook her head with a chuckle. "I just assumed you were looking for a new place. But if you have a place to go, then it's no problem."

Everyone nodded as if what Sophia said explained my situation perfectly.

"You're right, Sophia. Andrew is living there at the moment, and I am still paying the rent."

Her brows wrinkled as she lowered her coffee cup. "So, your ex-boyfriend, who cheated on you, gets to live in the apartment that you are paying for while you sleep in a tiny closet? That doesn't even make sense."

Harper opened her mouth but then closed it. I noticed the confusion on her face too. Lydia tilted her head as if working out a complicated problem.

"I know it's weird. I can't be in that apartment right now. Just the thought of entering it makes me physically sick."

"Then stop paying rent." Sophia blinked.

"Yeah, but then I'd have to go clear my stuff out, and that would mean me entering the apartment. I don't think I'm ready." I let out a breath.

"It's okay, Daisy. We get it. Right, Sophia?" Lydia nodded at her roommate.

Sophia pursed her lips. I knew she didn't agree. What I was doing went against everything Sophia stood for, but she was a friend. Despite her reservations, she nodded stiffly. That was the most anguished nod I had ever encountered.

Another cool gust of air washed over our almost completely silent table. The only noise was Harper slurping her coffee, followed by noises of relief.

"Do you plan to get your stuff today or tomorrow? I'm just asking out of curiosity." Sophia picked at her fingernail.

"I'm going back, not to get my stuff, but to live there. I'm paying the rent, anyway. It's not like Andrew contributes to that."

There was silence once more. Not even a slurp from Harper.

I knew my friends cared for me and couldn't understand why I was letting Andrew stay at my place. If I was being honest, I didn't know either. The thought of confronting Andrew again and entering that place made my skin crawl. It hadn't even been a full two days yet.

"I just need some time to process everything. Then I'm going back and kicking him out. He's probably out anyway, living with Angelica."

"No—" Lydia blurted out and reached across the table for my arm.

"No, what?"

"Angelica? He slept with your boss?" Sophia turned in her wooden chair toward me.

"Oh my god, what a bitch," Harper said, bringing her hand to her mouth.

For a moment, I hadn't known if Harper was shocked or about to throw up, though it was possibly a little of both.

"I hadn't told them who Andrew slept with," Lydia mumbled as she sat back in her chair.

Ugh, it felt like I was reliving Friday night all over again. I explained to them what I walked in on and even about the Chinese food on my foot.

"I don't know if I can ever eat that food again," I said, hating that Andrew ruined Szechuan chicken for me.

"You're going to quit on Monday, right?" Sophia asked.

I groaned. She would not understand—no one would—and that was fine. I knew my friends wanted the best for me. Working for a harpy who seduced your boyfriend wasn't a good thing. I knew that. Logically.

But fuck my boss and my ex if they were going to take my passion away from me. I loved helping animals. Where else was I going to do that and be able to pay my bills? Nowhere, unless I moved far away from my family and friends.

And that wasn't an option.

"I need more coffee." I stood purposefully, ignoring Sophia's question.

I couldn't explain my choices while the pain was raw. Not now.

A line had formed, so I stood, refusing to glance back at the table of women who judged me. My heart was broken, and at the moment, I felt totally alone. Was I being pathetic and only feeling sorry for myself? Yes. But damn it, I wanted to wallow.

A smell filled my nose that wasn't coffee, but it was something familiar. It was spicy, with hints of citrus.

Someone stood behind me, but I was too down in the dumps to discover who had that amazing scent.

I got up to the front of the line and ordered. Once I turned to move to the other end of the counter, I saw who was behind me.

Cillian.

Warmth bloomed in my chest, and my lips curled into the first smile of the day.

The guy I thought hated me. The guy I had crushed on for so long. The guy who proved last night that he could ignite heat down to my core without our lips even touching.

He wasn't the guy I thought he was, and that was definitely a good thing.

"Hi, Cillian." My cheeks hurt as my smile widened.

His deep blue eyes flickered up to mine. The larger my grin became, the more his frown deepened.

"Can I take your order?" the barista with long, curly brown hair asked him.

He glanced up at her and shook his head. "I made a mistake coming in here," Cillian said and then turned to stare at me.

I gasped.

He walked toward the door, leaving without glancing back.

Did he regret kissing me?

8

CILLIAN

Stepping off the ice, I inhaled the scent of mildew mixed with sweat, and it made me smile. Someone needed to bottle that scent. I bet every hockey player would pay top dollar for it.

Aspen hobbled by, and I slapped him on the back. "Great practice."

He stopped and almost fell over. The guy had been playing hockey for a few years now and still had a hard time walking on his skates if he wasn't on the ice.

"You okay, Cillian?"

I threw my head back with a laugh. Nothing was going to get me down today. After the past weekend, I realized something. Hockey was my passion; it was the one thing I was put on this earth to do. I wasn't meant to be friends with everyone I met; I wasn't meant to be the best son. And I certainly wasn't here to be a love interest for anyone of the opposite sex.

My laughter died as I thought about that last part. I hated to admit it, but how Daisy reacted to me when her friend opened the closet door at her party hurt.

Shaking my head, I would not let that get me down. Hockey was my goal. If getting a chance at the team captain position meant I had to be the nice guy on the team, then I'd work my ass off being friendly to all my teammates.

Even when they played like crap, which Aspen totally did today.

"I'm great. Love that ice rink scent on a Monday." To punctuate my point, I inhaled so deeply, my nostrils sucked together.

"Were you hit in the head out on the ice?" Aspen pointed to the rink behind me.

"No. You were on my shift with me. Did it look like I got hit with the puck?"

He shrugged. "Did you get into a car accident after the party on Saturday?"

My jaw tightened. Why was being nice so hard? I was trying my best, but it wasn't good enough.

"No."

He shook his gloved hand. "I know. You're in love." Aspen tried to whistle, but it ended up sounding like a fart. "Hey, Teddy, get over here. Did you know Cillian has a girlfriend?"

I groaned. God, it was like I was back in middle school.

"I was just trying to be supportive. Compliment-ing—"

"Yeah, I bet," Teddy cut me off, leaning on Aspen. "I heard you did the dirty at the party in a closet with someone. Damn, you move fast. She's already your girlfriend?"

Teddy towered over Aspen and just about any player on the team. Because of it, he took any chance he could to prop his elbow on the player's shoulders. Aspen was the only guy who wasn't annoyed by it.

I removed my hockey gloves and rubbed the sweat from my brow. "No, she's not my girlfriend. Look, I was trying to pay Aspen a compliment about his work on the ice today, that's all. I said nothing about Saturday. You just assumed." I pointed at Aspen.

Teddy pursed his lips and shook his head. "If you are going around complimenting any of us, but especially Aspen, then you're in love or on the verge of death. And you don't look like you're dying to me."

They both laughed.

I let out a sigh. It was time to move on from those two goofballs. Glancing around, I saw one of our newest players, Liam. He was one of the reserve players, only playing when one of us was injured.

"Hey, Liam." I waved at him.

His eyes grew large, and he pointed to himself as if he wasn't sure I was talking to him.

"Yeah, you. I want to talk to you." I shuffled toward him when I heard someone yell by the locker room entrance.

Brian, the team captain, held up his hands. "Hey, guys, before we head in there, I just wanted to make an announcement."

Everyone quieted their voices. I was excited to hear what Brian had to say since he never showed up at the party on Saturday.

"Guys, I love you all. You are like brothers to me; you know that." His lower lip wobbled. "I just wanted to let you know before Coach tells you... I'm moving at the end of the season. I'm going to go play with Boston."

There were gasps, and a few people exclaimed, "No!"

Instead, I chose positivity. "Congratulations, Brian," I said with a smile.

Some heads turned my way, but I ignored them. Despite my setback with Aspen, I was going to keep up my kindness effort.

Brian nodded in my direction with a frown, then turned toward another guy, fist-pumping him.

Brian was great whenever we talked about hockey, but if I ever tried to strike up a conversation with him that didn't involve sports, I got the impression he didn't want to talk to me. I guessed he was like most of the players; they just didn't like me.

Boston was a better team than the Devils, but not by a lot. Sure, I'd miss Brian. He was a dominant player, and he had been with the team the longest out of everyone. But he also knew it was time to move on, and I was glad he was doing what was best for him. And, of course, I was elated I finally had a chance at team captain.

The players slowly made their way toward the locker room. Brian stood to the side, accepting everyone's warm sentiments. I wanted to go over and shake his hand, maybe even ask for some advice on how to be a great captain. Right as I was a few feet away from him, I heard my name being called.

I glanced over my shoulder and saw Coach waving me toward him. Turning, my skates dug into the soggy carpet as I walked over to Coach. He was leaning against the painted cement wall.

"Cillian, I want to talk to you before you head home." He nodded toward the locker room entrance. "Come to my office."

With that, he turned and walked through a metal door that led to his tiny office. It had a separate entrance from the locker room and a large window that overlooked the main locker area.

The coach sat on his black leather swivel chair behind a small pine desk. There was a chalkboard behind him and on the opposite wall, a corkboard with a bench underneath. I sat on the bench.

"Coach, I'm glad you asked to talk. I wanted a chance to tell you that I took your advice. I didn't hang out with the guys on Friday night like you suggested, but I went to a party on Saturday night for Jackson's sister's birthday. A lot of the teammates were there."

I shrugged. "I think I did a good job staying positive and complimenting the players today. Even with Brian after his announcement, I congratulated him." I pointed toward the window overlooking the players.

When I glanced back at Coach, I was surprised by what I saw. He shook his head as if I disappointed him.

I was confused. I did exactly as he said, yet he seemed upset.

"Cillian, I hate to say it, but I think it might be too little too late."

"What do you mean, too little too late? I did what you said and hung out with the guys. I've been nice to them and didn't make any comments when they made mistakes out on the ice today." I rolled my shoulders.

I should've kept my mouth shut, but fuck it. I did what the coach wanted, and it still wasn't good enough.

"I can point out ten mistakes by at least three players that happened today. Which brings me to something that's really bothering me. Why am I having a talk with you when they're not? It's obvious they aren't that good."

"Cillian, I'm going to stop you right there. Those mistakes can be corrected; that's what practice is for. And I have talked to those players to give them individual advice. They have taken on personal coaches and physical therapists to work on those issues. They can work on the technique."

I stood. "I can work on being nice. It's just being complimentary. That's not very hard."

"No," he shook his head, "it's harder."

"What?" How could being nicer be more difficult than training and playing on a professional-level hockey team?

"The reason you are in here is because I had another complaint about you today."

"Complaint? I didn't even realize you had one complaint about me. I thought it was because of the nickname they gave me."

"I didn't want to have to tell you this because you're an excellent player. You're one of the best forward centers I've ever worked with. But if your teammates constantly complain about you, and you're getting penalties during games, that becomes an issue I can't ignore."

He let out a deep sigh. "The past two years, complaints about you from the players have increased. Every player gets a complaint here and there. But over the past few years, they have doubled for you. The penalties this past year have increased too. Ever since your mom passed, you haven't let go. Instead of going through the grieving process, you've stopped at anger and have refused to move forward."

I was shocked at what was coming out of the coach's mouth. How could he mention her when he knew what she went through? I missed her, but that had nothing to do with how I was as a player.

My nostrils flared as I took a step toward his desk. "You don't know how I feel about my mom... about her death."

"Cillian, remember, I was the one who took the call."

How could I forget? It was the biggest mistake of my life going to that game.

"Don't you think I regret going? You knew it was a mistake, and you let me go anyway."

He held up his hands. "There was no talking you out of it. Look, I'm so sorry you weren't there when your mom passed. But please, stop blaming me, the team, strangers on the street. But most importantly, stop blaming yourself."

I ran my fingers through my hair, hating the conversation.

He wanted me to be nice, and then he brought up my mom.

"Of course I blame myself. I should have been there for her. I was her only child. All she wanted was to see me before she died."

Instead, I was off playing a game in another city because somehow, I believed if I won, if I told my mom I won, that it would be okay. That would make her better. Deep down I knew that couldn't cure cancer, but I was desperate to make her smile. When I won, her grin always lit up a room.

God, I missed her.

I cleared my throat. "I want to be captain."

Coach's head jerked back. "What?"

"You heard me, Coach. I want to be team captain. I've earned it, and I'm the oldest player on the team."

"One of the oldest. Jackson is also thirty-two."

"Yes, well, once Brian leaves, then typically the oldest player becomes captain."

"It's also voted on, Cillian. The players vote who becomes captain, and what have we been talking about?" He waved around the room. "You've had complaints from team members. Do you think they're really going to vote for you to be team captain? I'm discussing possibly letting you go. You realize the seriousness of this?"

I did.

"I still want to be captain. And if I am nice and the players stop complaining about me, then you can't let me go, right?"

I held my breath. How could I be considered for team captain if I had no team to play on?

"Of course. My job is to make sure the Devils are a solid team. It's not just about skill; it's about being a family. If you are serious, Cillian, and the players stop complaining, then I won't let you go. But you have to try."

"Whatever it takes. Whatever you think I should do—"

My phone ringing in my pocket cut me off.

Coach told everyone no cell phones on the rink. I knew I shouldn't have my phone in my pocket while I was playing.

But he made an exception for me. After what happened with my mother, he let me keep the phone on vibrate during practice.

I lifted it out and saw it was my father.

"Dad, what's wrong?" He only ever called me once before in my life—the day my mother died. He couldn't get ahold of me, so he ended up calling

Coach that day. "Are you okay?" I asked, trying to hold back the fear in my voice.

"Yes, Cillian, I'm fine. But there's been an accident."

"What? What's going on?"

It was like my mother all over again. My father could obviously talk, so the accident wasn't that bad, but he could have had a concussion or internal bleeding. I had to get out of here.

I covered the phone and turned to Coach. "I have to go. There's been an accident."

He nodded and waved me off.

I moved quickly into the locker room, thankful most of the guys had dressed and left. It was always too loud to hear a phone call when all the players were around.

"What happened? Tell me everything." I tried to balance the phone pressed between my shoulder and neck as I removed my skates.

"It's Arizona... He got run over by a car. He's been in surgery for over an hour now."

9

DAISY

Work had been brutal. Not only was the clinic slammed with back-to-back appointments, but several of our pet owners already knew Andrew and I broke up. One pitfall of living in a small town: gossip.

It was so busy that I didn't even have time to chat with Diana, our receptionist, until late in the day.

"Daisy," Diana exclaimed as I walked into the waiting room and leaned against her desk. "Glad to see you. How was your weekend?" Her lips turned up into a grin as she twisted a lock of her purple hair around her finger.

I liked Diana. She was the most positive person I knew. I wondered what positive spin she'd put on my weekend exploits.

"Just my boyfriend sleeping with Angelica in our bedroom. Then me couch surfing, so my back is ready to give out."

Diana's hair twirling stopped, and her matching purple smile slowly faded as she made an O with her lips. "Is that a joke? If it is, I don't get it."

I frowned. It wasn't her fault Andrew was a boob. I shouldn't be snarky, trying to burst her happy little bubble.

"Sorry. I had an awful weekend. Andrew and I broke up, and Angelica is now sleeping with him. So, there's that. I've been sleeping in a closet at my friend's place. I thought it was a cute idea on Saturday, but it really isn't. Sleeping in a closet is not adorable in any way."

"I remember when I was young, I'd clean out my closet and set up pillows for a cool space that was just my own. I'm one of seven brothers and sisters. It really was my only private space in that house," Diana said.

"Yikes," I said a little too quickly. "Sorry, I mean, uh..." I was trying to think of a happy spin but really couldn't come up with anything.

She waved me off. "No, it wasn't great. We never had enough food, and the only one of us who never got hand-me-downs to wear was our oldest brother. Yes, even the girls had to wear his clothes. So, one day, I made a space in my closet and pretended I was an only child." She sighed and gazed off into the distance.

After a moment, Diana snapped out of her youthful memory. "Were you able to fit a mattress in there?"

"Lydia had a spare mattress—one of those blow-up things. It just fit, filling the entire space. A bed in a room with no walking space, kind of like sleeping in a deep coffin." I shook my head. "I thought it would be cozy; that's why I suggested it."

Diana held up her hand and started ticking off her fingers. "Okay, so several points. I'll come back to the bed in a closet situation later. First point, why are you here?"

"This is my job. I work here."

She tilted her head. "But you said Angelica slept with Andrew. Why would you still be working for a woman who did that?"

Both Jackson and Lydia had been talking to me all weekend about quitting. Jackson even said he'd pay my rent until I got another job. I, of course, told him no. He needed that money after what Katie did to him in the divorce.

"I want to be a veterinarian so badly. Where else can I go? Trust me, I thought about it a lot, Diana. But this is my passion. I love working with animals." I waved around the small waiting room with plastic folding chairs lining the walls, a ficus tree in one corner, and an end table topped with *Pet Fancy* magazines in the other corner.

"I understand that, Daisy. I hear what the pet owners say when they're sitting here in the lobby. They go on and on about you and how you really care about their pets." She leaned in, lowering her voice. "I think you're better than Angelica." Diana sat up straight and continued, "I would not want to work for the woman sleeping with my ex... I just wouldn't." She held up her hands. "But that's just me. I'm not saying you're a bad person for staying."

I frowned. She was judging me, and I knew I deserved it. She was so right—as were Jackson and Lydia. Even yesterday at the coffee shop, I wouldn't admit it to her, but what Sophia told me made sense.

Closing my eyes, I took a deep breath before exhaling. I couldn't believe I walked in here today.

"You know what, Diana? You're right. I should quit. I need to walk out that door right this minute." I pointed to the wooden door separating Fitzlee Street from the clinic. "Even if it means I have to take a job over at that gaudy, exclusive resort, The Blue Spot, with all their spoiled, billionaire guests."

I smiled and felt a rush of happiness. Slamming the counter with my palm, I said, "I'll do it. Yes, they're billionaires, but I bet a lot of them have pets. They will need somebody to watch their pets as they go about doing their billionaire things. So, I'll be the most overqualified pet sitter in the world."

I swallowed. The idea of leaving felt like a tremendous relief, but ending up as a pet sitter didn't.

Diana gave me her usual peppy smile. "That sounds great."

As the seconds ticked by and the thought of pet sitting for out-of-touch wealthy people sank in, I doubted myself.

Suddenly, the idea sounded terrible. But what could I do? That was what Andrew and Angelica did to me.

I better get used to picking up dog poop and hunting down specialized, gourmet, locally-sourced dog food.

Sucking on my lower lip, I shook my head. "I can't do it. I didn't go to school and take the veterinarian exams just so I could be a nanny for overly pampered pets."

Diana sighed, resting her chin on her clasped hands. "I get it. You love these animals. And you treat them well. I just wish there was a way you could fire Angelica."

"Yes," I nodded, "I thought the same thing. When she says she's got a doctor appointment, it's code for going to bang Andrew."

Diana lifted her head. "She's the one who said if she caught us lying about not being at work, we'd be fired instantly."

"That's why I think she should fire herself."

"Yeah. It's only fair."

I snapped my fingers. "I'm going to do it."

Diana tilted her head. "What?"

"I'm going to march into Angelica's office and tell her she needs to fire herself."

"You're going to do what now?"

I pushed my hands on my hips, standing tall. "When I get done with Angelica, she'll be the one running out of this place... not me."

"Uh, Daisy, we were only playing around. Just letting you get your anger out about Angelica. You know she will not fire herself. This is *her* clinic."

It was too late for formalities. I had a plan.

"I have been pushed around too much by that woman and Andrew. Taken advantage of by them. It's time one of them pays. And when she's gone, I can be the veterinarian, no longer just the animal tech."

My sneakers squeaked against the beige vinyl floor tiles. Diana called out to me, but I ignored her as I made my way down the back hallway to Angelica's office.

I stood in front of the closed white door and pushed my shoulders back. Lifting my fist, I pounded on her door.

"Who is it?" her high-pitched voice screeched.

"It's me. Daisy. I need to speak with you."

"Make it quick," she said, sounding annoyed.

My teeth clenched. I felt like an idiot for looking up to her when I first started, idolizing a successful, independent business owner, doing what she loved. It wasn't until I worked for her that her beautiful façade cracked and slowly crumbled.

I found out her ex-husband set up her clinic, and then they divorced. Why didn't that marriage last? Because she cheated on him. From what Diana told me, he worshiped her, and she just used him for his money.

Then I saw the way she treated the animals. Each one was an annoyance she tried to help as quickly as possible. And by help, I meant make me do the exam and pass on the results to her while she spent one minute in the exam room with the pet owner explaining the problem. And if the owner had questions, she gave them a pamphlet.

She actually used a timer on her phone, and once that timer went off, she was done dealing with the pet.

I grasped the brass knob and turned, pushing open the door. She held her phone in her hand, tapping away at it, never looking up.

"Angelica, we need to talk."

"I got that, Daisy. I'm not deaf. What do you need to talk about right now when I'm obviously busy?" She waved her hand at her phone.

It was amusing; she thought playing Lollipop Smash was her way of being busy. I bet she thought I didn't know about her game addiction.

"What level are you on?"

"Level one hundred and fifty-two—" She stopped herself and lowered the phone. "I just opened the game right before you came in here."

I folded my arms over my chest. "Sure."

Angelica leaned back in her white leather chair. "I am assuming you didn't come in here to talk about games? What do you want?"

I lifted my arm and pointed at her, secretly hoping she didn't notice how my hand shook ever so slightly. "You're fired." My voice was wobbly as I gave her my answer.

Her eyes widened. "Fired? Me?" She threw her head back with a loud chuckle.

"You were the one who lied about going to doctor appointments when you were really seeing Andrew.

According to your own policy, you should be fired on the spot."

Her laughter died, and she straightened. "Here's the problem with that logic, Daisy. I pay the bills. The clinic is in my name. If I am fired, who will pay your salary? Where will the animals go once the rent isn't paid to the building? If I go, so does this clinic."

Shit. I hadn't thought of that. Diana mentioned that this was Angelica's business. I was too worked up at the time to realize what that really meant.

She gave a cartoonish frown and stood, walking around her black desk to stand next to me. Slipping her hand around my back, Angelica pulled me into a side hug. It was nauseating.

"If you don't want me firing you, I suggest you get over this hang-up you have about me being with Andrew."

My eyes burned, and I knew tears weren't far off from falling. I took a deep breath and willed myself not to cry. She didn't deserve to witness my pain.

"I just found out on Friday."

Thankfully, she let me go as she moved around to face me. "Exactly. You had the entire weekend to deal with whatever feelings you had for him. My first boyfriend dumped me for my best friend my senior year in high school. It took me all of two hours to move on to her brother."

Ugh, she really was the worst.

Her phone beeped behind me. She ran around the desk in her three-inch heels and tight gray pencil skirt to grab it.

"Oh, good." Her red lips twisted into a satisfied grin. "I have a doctor's appointment. It shouldn't be long. You can take over while I'm out."

"Really? You're still using the doctor appointment excuse? You realize I know you're going to see Andrew."

Grabbing her puffy gold coat and placing it on her shoulders, Angelica shook her head. "It's a doctor appointment. I'll be gone about fifteen minutes, max."

I rolled my eyes as she sashayed out her office door.

Groaning, I went back into the waiting room. It was still empty, but the cool air lingered from Angelica having just left.

"Did you actually fire her?" Diana blinked at the door.

"No. You were right. It was silly nonsense. This place would close if she wasn't here."

"Then where did she go?"

"Doctor's appointment." I rolled my eyes as Diana snorted. "What doctor appointment is only going to take fifteen minutes?"

"Yup."

"And I know from experience, fifteen minutes is more than enough time for sex with Andrew. She could squeeze in a shower if she wanted with all the time she'd have left once they finished."

Diana's head fell back with laughter.

The bell on the front door rang as it opened. I expected Angelica to walk through, telling us the doctor appointment was shorter than she thought.

But it was much worse.

Katie walked through the door. Her orange-tipped fingers held a leash to a small black puppy.

"Katie, what are you doing here?" I asked Jackson's ex-wife.

She pushed her bleach-blond waves off her shoulder and sneered, "I should ask you the same question."

I rubbed the spot between my brows. A sharp pain seemed to always strike whenever Katie was around.

"You knew I worked for a veterinarian."

She stepped farther inside, pulling the puppy with her. The dog yelped and placed its butt down on the floor, refusing to move.

Katie groaned, throwing her head back like an overdramatic teenager. "This dog is so annoying."

"Then why do you have it? I can't imagine you volunteered to dog-sit. That would mean you'd have to help people. Aren't you allergic to helping?" I tilted my head.

"Ha, ha. No, Daisy. If you must know, I just got this puppy for Lucas."

I blinked. I didn't remember Jackson mentioning Lucas getting a puppy. Since I was his sister and worked for a vet, I thought I'd be the first person he told.

"Jackson agreed to a puppy?"

Dogs weren't cheap, and my brother was struggling. Why would he agree to a pet?

"He doesn't know." Her bubblegum-pink lips gave a smile that reminded me of the Grinch.

That pain throbbed between my brows again.

"He's the one taking care of Lucas, so he needs to know. And why would you get a puppy? It was too hard for you to take care of your own child. What makes you think you can care for a dog?"

I knew that was a low blow, but she deserved it.

Her nose flared. "I can take care of a dog. And my son too. In fact, I plan to request sole custody—"

Right at that moment, the door to the clinic flew open, and an older man stood there, holding a limp dog in his arms.

"Please, help him. A car hit him."

10

CILLIAN

I ran into the veterinarian clinic on Fitzlee Street. "Where is Arizona?"

The waiting room was small and smelled like wet fur and urine. A blond woman stood at the receptionist's desk with a puppy at her feet. When I saw my dad, I went over to him.

My father stood from a chair set against the wall and held up his hands. "He's with the vet now."

I ran my fingers through my hair. "How did this happen?"

My father let out a breath, shaking his head. "I took him for a walk, and I guess I didn't have a good grip on the leash, so—"

"Do you mind keeping it down? I need to make an appointment for my puppy." The woman with the puppy frowned at my father.

"What?"

"As I told you when you came in over an hour ago, the vet can't see you right now. And even if you leave and come back in another hour she still can't just perform a neutering via walk-in." The purple haired woman at the receptionist desk said the blonde.

It had been a dreadful day. I spent the entire morning and most of the afternoon trying with my team, only for the coach to tell me he might fire me.

Then my beloved dog was hit by a car.

I was at my breaking point. Turning to the blonde woman, I walked up to her and lowered my head into her face. "You know they have this invention now called phones. You can use it to call the vet and make an appointment. That way, my father explaining to me how my dog got hit by a car won't be too much for your sensitive ears."

She pursed her lips, and I wondered if her face would crack with the amount of makeup she had on. Right when I thought she was going to yell at me, the woman's eyes widened.

Her entire demeanor changed. She stood straight, pushing out her chest and licking her lips. "You're that hockey player, Cillian Walsh. Aren't you?"

My jaw tightened as I took a step back. "Yes."

Her fingertip, with the ugliest shade of orange nail polish I had ever seen, reached up to my chest and tapped me three times. "I. Knew. It."

"Congratulations." I turned and headed over to the seat next to my dad.

But before I could move, her hand reached over and grabbed my shoulder. I thought about slipping off my black leather jacket but didn't. I turned back to face the smiling clown.

"I used to be married to Jackson. You know, your teammate, Jackson Haynes. I'm actually making an appointment for his puppy."

"You married Jackson?" I raised a brow at her.

She giggled, and I assume she was trying to appear cute, but it had the same effect as nails on a chalkboard.

"You're so funny. Instead of going after Jackson, I should have turned my attention on *you*."

I narrowed my eyes. "I have never seen you before in my life. If you don't mind, I have to talk to my dad about—"

"Oh, I don't mind." She took a step closer until her cheap metallic coat brushed against mine. "I don't mind anything you want to do... to me." She winked.

"Oh god," my father groaned.

I placed my hands on her shoulders and took a step back. When she tried to move closer, I held her in place. "You seem to think all hockey players are as gullible and dim-witted as my teammate, but I am not." I let go of her and waved my arm up and down her body. "I want nothing to do with this."

"Whatever," she said. "You don't even know what you just walked away from."

My shoulders sagged. I glanced up at my dad, who was shaking his head at me. He wanted me to leave it alone, but he should have known by now I couldn't do that.

"Jackson seemed happy when he walked away from you, so I feel no loss there."

"I left him." She scooped up her puppy that squirmed in her arms. "He couldn't handle me. I had to find happiness with other men."

She wore a smug look on her face. The woman was actually proud of cheating on Jackson. I wasn't a fan of him, but no one deserved to be cheated on—not to mention, he had a son.

That was when it clicked. She was the mother of that little boy. At that moment, I felt sorry for Jackson. That he had to put up with her for the rest of his life.

"Knowing that you cheat on the men you're with really isn't helping your case with me. Be gone, banshee..." I waved her off, "and take your little dog too."

She groaned but took my advice and left.

There was a noise from the hallway. Daisy slowly appeared, clapping at me. I sucked in a breath when I saw her. Her cheeks were flushed, and the way she smiled at me... I felt a twitch in my cock.

"I needed that after the day I had."

The way she said it had me picturing her naked in my bed.

Stop, Cillian. Your dog may be dead, and you're imagining the vet naked. Not the time.

"God, it was so good, Daisy," the receptionist with purple and black hair swooned. "You should have seen Katie's expression. She was *pissed*."

The two women chatted about the woman who left.

89

"Excuse me." I waved my hand at them. "But what about my dog?"

Daisy tilted her head. "Dog?"

"Yes, Arizona. My father brought him in here because he was in an accident."

"Ah, yes. Arizona." She waved for me to follow her toward the hallway.

I turned to my dad and asked if he wanted to come. He got up, and we both moved down the small hallway and into a room with a large metal table in the center.

My heart pounded in my ears. Arizona wasn't here. When I glanced up at Daisy, she frowned, clasping her hands together.

Oh no, did he die?

"Where's Arizona?"

My father placed his hand on my shoulder and gave a comforting squeeze.

"Arizona is fine. He's resting in our recovery area," Daisy said with a quick smile.

"Thank God." I let out a breath I hadn't realized I was holding. "It wasn't as bad as I thought."

Daisy raised her finger. "I assumed your father told you."

My head bobbed between her and my dad. "Told me what?"

"I had to amputate Arizona's leg."

My head felt light. I shook it, trying to focus.

"Amputate..." I murmured, hoping it would make sense in my head.

"Like I said, your dog is fine, and the operation was a success. He is still asleep from the anesthesia I gave him. But the wound didn't seem to be infected, thanks to your father's quick actions."

I reached up and placed my hand over my dad's. There were so many thoughts swirling around my head. Who hit my dog, and where did they go? How would Arizona cope without the use of one of his legs?

I took a deep breath. "When can we take him home?"

"I would like Arizona to stay here for the next two days so we can monitor him and make sure the incision is healing properly."

"I should have been there..."

"Son, you were busy at practice."

I turned to my father. "I know, but Mom entrusted me with Arizona, and I was busy *again*."

My father's big blue eyes softened. "I understand. But you can't be there for everyone all the time. Arizona is fine, just like the vet said."

"Unfortunately, pets get hit by cars all the time, Cillian," Daisy said. "A lot of dogs have escaped from owners, only to run into the street and get hit. It happens. No one is to blame."

"Someone is..." I tensed my jaw. "The driver." I turned to my dad. "What happened to the driver? Did they just speed off?"

My father shook his head. "No. How do you think Arizona and I got here? His name is Sam, and he's just a kid."

My eyes widened. "A child was driving a car?"

"Son, stop being ignorant. He's a teenager. Told me he had only been driving for six months, and he was worried his parents would take away his license. So, he dropped us off here and said he needed to go talk to them."

"He shouldn't have been out driving by himself," I muttered.

I heard my dad groan. I didn't care if he didn't agree; that boy could have killed my dog.

"He seemed like a good kid, just made a mistake that, really, anyone could have made. Arizona darted right in front of his car. It wasn't the kid's fault."

I raised my finger and pointed at my dad. "If he knew how to handle that car better—"

There was a knock on the door.

"Come in," Daisy said, and I noticed the look of relief on her face.

The door creaked open, and the purple-haired receptionist popped her head in. "Sam Gould and his father, Thomas Gould, are in the waiting room wishing to speak with all of you about Arizona."

"Great," Daisy said a little too enthusiastically. "We'll be right out."

The scent of lilacs filled my nose as Daisy brushed past me. For a moment, all my anger at what happened to Arizona disappeared, and my heart pumped a little faster as I watched the vet walk out the door.

"I told you he was a good kid. A bad one wouldn't show up here."

I pursed my lips and glanced over and my father. "She also said his father is here. I bet the father made him come. Probably looking to sue us for a tiny dent in his car."

My dad sighed as he followed me out of the room and down the hallway toward the waiting room. "Cillian, I love you, but you have to stop thinking the worst of people. Not everyone is out to get you."

Yes, they were.

There was a tall man in a business suit with thick black hair who looked about a decade older than me. Next to him stood a much younger and skinnier version of him in jeans, a flannel button-up shirt, and puffy navy-blue coat. The younger one kept tapping his sneakers on the floor.

"Hello, I'm Thomas Gould, Sam's dad. When I heard about what happened to your dog—"

"Arizona, Dad. The dog's name is Arizona." Sam's eyes shifted from the ground to his father and then back to the ground.

"Yes, Arizona." His smile stiffened. "I insisted we come right over to see how the dog, I mean... Arizona is doing."

I took a step forward and folded my arms. "Well, Thomas, I'm Cillian, Arizona's owner. He's not well. It seems with your son's driving skills that his—"

"The operation was a success," Daisy said, cutting me off.

I glared over my shoulder at her.

She ignored me, and with a wide grin that showed off her dimples, she continued, "Yes, as I was telling

Cillian and Mr. Walsh, if it weren't for Sam's excellent driving to get Arizona to me right away, the wound could have become infected. Things could have been much worse for Arizona, but thankfully, he is resting and will recover."

Sam placed his hand over his chest and let out a breath. "Thank goodness. I was so worried."

"As was I when Sam told me. We lost our dog, Phineas, last year to a hit and run."

"I'm sorry," both my dad and Daisy said in unison.

My father nudged my arm. I grumbled but finally said, "I am sorry too. But what the vet didn't tell you was Arizona's leg had to be amputated. He'll probably never walk again."

The father and son stood there with their mouths hanging open.

"The dog will walk again. That's not a problem." Daisy pursed her lips as she stepped up to me. "I haven't spoken with Cillian about physical therapy, but dog amputees walk all the time."

"Yeah, Son." My father gave a nod that told me I should keep my mouth shut.

"It was a terrible accident, and I came here to make sure that we covered all the veterinarian bills. If the dog needs physical therapy, we will pay for that too." His father looked over at his son. "Isn't that right, Sam?"

The boy nodded. "Yes, Dad."

I suspected the father had a lot of work lined up for his son to pay those bills.

I stood there for a moment and watched them. My dad was right; I was assuming the worst in people. These people weren't trying to take advantage of me; the boy wasn't shirking his responsibility.

"Thanks, but that's unnecessary—"

"All we need is half the vet bill. The rest we can take care of," my dad said, surprising me.

He was the one who let things slide, not me.

"Are you sure? Sam will do what it takes to help," Thomas said.

I glanced back at my dad and then at the boy. "How about some farm work?" I asked. "Would Sam be open to some work on the farm? We'd pay him, of course."

The father looked stunned but nodded.

It was time for my dad to step foot on the farm. He'd been gone too long, and I thought it would be a good way for him to get out more and finally do what he always loved.

"I'm going to head back with the vet to find out about the physical therapy." I threw my thumb over my shoulder. "Dad, why don't you talk to Sam about the farm?"

I knew my dad wouldn't ask anyone to help with the farm. The last thing he wanted to do was go back—not because he didn't like the farm, but because it reminded him of my mom.

He hid from her memory on a recliner in my living room.

But if he thought it was a way to work off a punishment for a kid to learn a lesson, I knew my dad would be all for it. He came from the old school of parenting—you learn life lessons through manual labor.

I turned to Daisy and waved toward the hallway. She seemed a bit confused but nodded, and we moved back to the room we were in earlier.

Once she had closed the door, she turned to me. "Arizona will need some physical therapy once he's healed enough to move around."

I nodded. "That seems fine. Do you think he will walk?"

I knew they had advances now to help animals move around, like little wheeled carts, but I wanted my dog to run and get upstairs without having to rely on someone. Maybe that made me selfish, but after losing my mom, it wasn't just my dad and me who suffered. I had never seen an animal grieve until I witnessed Arizona's sadness. It broke my heart, and I vowed to never to let him suffer like that again.

"Yes. With the right therapy, Arizona should have no problem using his three other legs to compensate."

"Okay." I nodded with a sense of relief.

"I have been trained to help animals, though I am not technically a physical therapist. But I can do that for Arizona."

"Aren't you busy here? You're the vet."

She winced. "Actually, I'm the animal technician. Dr. Angelica Goode is the vet here, but she's at a doctor's appointment." Daisy rolled her eyes.

"Wait." I took a step back. "You're not even the vet... and you *operated* on my dog? Did my dad know that?"

"Yes, but—"

"But nothing. You don't have the experience. You could have killed him."

"I'm an actual licensed veterinarian. Having gone to school and passed all the state exams, I got my license two years ago. But at this clinic, Dr. Goode felt it was necessary to give me the title of animal tech. I only step in as veterinarian when she is out."

I felt slightly better that she was certified, but I couldn't help but be suspicious as to why she hadn't told me earlier.

"Aren't there other physical therapists I could go to?" I wasn't feeling comfortable with Daisy helping my dog anymore.

She stepped over to the small counter that held metal jars and a small sink. She grabbed a piece of paper that was lying in the middle of the counter.

"Here is a list of physical therapists within a one-hundred-mile radius."

I plucked the paper from her hand and glanced over the towns, my eyes widening at the nearest location. "One hundred...?" I pointed to the one circled in red ink at the top of the page. "This therapist is in Scottsville. That's sixty miles away."

"Yes, I was going to suggest that one if you refused my service." She mumbled something else, but I didn't catch it. "That's one drawback of living in such a rural location... nothing is ever close."

I thought about Arizona and if he could deal with such a long car ride.

"How often would he need to go?"

"About once a week."

She had helped Arizona and saved his life. It wasn't like she didn't know what she was doing. Technically, Daisy was a veterinarian.

I was about to agree to her proposal about physical therapy when the door swung open. In the doorway stood a tall, buxom woman with cascading black curls that fell over her shoulders.

"Daisy, I heard what happened. How dare you perform an operation without my permission!"

Daisy rubbed the spot between her eyebrows. "I tried to call you, but you didn't answer, and I couldn't wait for—"

"That's no excuse. As of this moment, you're fired."

My mouth fell open, as did Daisy's. I said something to defend Daisy, but the woman slammed the door.

"What the fuck just happened?" I blurted out.

"My bad day from Friday extended to Monday," she murmured, though it seemed more for her own benefit.

I moved toward Daisy, but she held up her hand. "Just know that Arizona is fine. All he needs now is to heal. Make an appointment with Diana in the waiting room to pick him up on Wednesday. I have to go hide in a deep coffin filled with a back-breaking air mattress."

She moved to the door, let out a breath, and opened it. Before I could say anything, she was gone, and I was alone in the room.

While I was glad Arizona would be fine, I couldn't help but wonder if Daisy being fired was my fault.

11

DAISY

"Barkeep, pour me another." I slammed the wooden table and caused it to rattle.

"My name is Susanna." She tapped at the silver pitcher in her hand. "And this is our dark roast from the French press."

I had been jobless for two days, and I felt like I was lost in a horrible nightmare. One where my boss got my man and the job of my dreams, while I swigged coffee like it was some magic elixir that would cure all that ailed me.

"Whatever you want to call it, I need another. I've had a terrible week."

She nodded and gave me a sympathetic smile. "Once I fill your cup, I've got to go back to the customers waiting in line. I can't keep coming over here to pour you another. If you want more, just head up to the counter."

I ignored everything she said and responded with, "You've got a job. That's the important thing." I slashed my finger in the air but somehow swung widely and knocked my biscuit onto the floor.

"Honey, you obviously have had an awful week. How about I give you another biscuit on the house?"

"Thank you. You're a good person, and I appreciate you. Your boss is lucky to have you. Lucky..." I whispered the last part.

"Is there somebody I can call for you? Do you need a ride home? I know that this is just a coffee shop, and I haven't witnessed you drinking, but the way you're acting..."

I waved my hands at her. "No, no, I'm fine. I'm just going to keep using your restroom for a while. I drank a lot of coffee."

"That was a little too much information for me. I'm heading back to the register."

The barista with the brown curly hair walked off, and I felt a sense of joy for her because she had a job.

I didn't.

She got to do what she loved—being surrounded by coffee. I bet she loved it here. I didn't know her, but I felt like I knew her.

Right as I was about to lift the dark roast to my lips so I could try to forget my troubles, I saw a man with an enormous bouquet of beautiful flowers.

Smiling, I thought to myself, there was a good guy. Obviously buying that bouquet for the person he loved. Whoever those flowers were for, they were lucky to have him in their life.

As I was staring at the colorful flora, his head turned my way. My grin faded into a deep frown. He wasn't a good man... He was the worst.

"Daisy. So funny running into you here," he said, stepping toward my table.

"Hi, Andrew. I didn't recognize you with that gigantic bouquet you have in your hand. I thought you were deathly allergic to flowers."

He chuckled. "Why would you think that?"

"I don't know. Maybe because you never once got me flowers. *Ever*."

"That can't be right. I'm sure I bought you flowers at some point..." He snapped his fingers. "That birthday of yours. I got you some daisies. I thought it was funny. You know, with your name being Daisy and all."

"Hilarious." My sarcasm was so thick, it dripped to the floor. "You didn't buy them. You saw them in somebody's garden and picked them for me. I remember because I kept commenting how the dirt from the roots was falling all over the floor."

He waved me off. "The point is, I got you flowers."

"You're a real winner," I mumbled to myself.

"What?" He leaned closer, but right as I was about to lay into the cheater—remind him he was sleeping in the apartment I paid for—another person walked up to my table.

If my day couldn't be filled enough with nightmares past, Katie snapped her fingers in my face.

"Hey. You screwed up." She flashed her teeth like a hyena, which made sense, since she looked like the human form of one.

"Please, Katie, join in on the discussion. Next topic will be, how best to ruin Daisy's life. I'll start." I held up my finger. "Kidnap her in the night and leave her in a wolf's den. Because I feel that is a likely scenario, given how my life has gone lately."

Katie frowned and tilted her head. "You're insane. You better not infect my son with your crazy."

"She's not crazy, just stressed. Isn't that right, Daisy? Every time I thought you were losing it when we were together, you'd explain that you were just overworked."

I pressed an imaginary button on the table and made a loud buzzing sound. Many people in the shop turned to glance over at me.

"You're both wrong. I can't be overworked when I have no job. And I can't be crazy because it's you two who are crazy."

Or maybe I was going off the deep end? I was pretending to press buzzers and letting these two idiots talk to me.

"Whatever. The reason I'm mad is because you screwed up my appointment for the puppy. It was supposed to be today, but that woman there with her long black curls kept telling me she was too busy. I need to make sure everything is okay with the puppy to surprise Lucas."

I groaned. I had completely forgotten about the puppy thing.

"Did you tell Jackson yet?" I asked, lifting my eyes to her.

Her head shot back. "What? No. It's my gift to give. If I let him know, he'll probably tell Lucas the puppy was his idea. I can't have that." She pursed her bright pink lips.

"But he'll have to take care of the puppy when you aren't around. He needs to know." I rubbed at the spot between my brows.

Why did life hate me so much?

She tapped her foot. "I'll tell him after the vet appointment. Okay?"

I nodded.

"So, can you come and look at the dog?"

"I just said I was jobless. How can I check out the puppy? I am no longer a veterinarian." Just saying that out loud caused my heart to sink as bile crept up the back of my throat. My dream of helping animals flickered out in a heartbeat.

I noticed she hadn't even given it a name yet. I wondered if Katie was incapable of love and affection.

"Then what am I supposed to do? I can't keep the puppy much longer. Antonio is allergic to animals."

"Antonio? Who the hell is Antonio?"

Her eyes widened. "Oh, uh… he's my, uh… my maid. That's right. He's a maid. And I can't have the help unfit to work for me."

"Wow, you can afford a maid while not having a child to raise, yet my bother can only afford a small one-bedroom apartment while taking care of his son. Remind me again, Katie, what do you do for a living?"

Her eyes darted around the room. I had caught her. Deep down, I knew she was using my brother. He paid her alimony while he cared for their child, and she did nothing.

"Those flowers are beautiful," Katie said, batting her lashes at Andrew.

Was there a man she wouldn't flirt with?

"Thank you. They're for someone else, but I think this red rose has your name on it." Andrew pulled out the flower and presented it to Katie.

She gasped, placing her hand on her chest and the fakest expression of shock on her face. "Really? That's so sweet. I heard you two broke up."

Of course she did. It surprised me that our breakup wasn't the headline in the local paper this past weekend.

"Yes. It's been so hard for me." Andrew lowered his head as if holding back tears.

That weasel.

I was about to ask him if he was referring to his penis when he said hard, because of what I witnessed the night we broke up, when Katie said, "You poor man. And here you are, defending her after what she did to you..."

"Wait, a minute—" I stood, about to correct Katie when Andrew cut me off.

"I just felt so ignored."

My mouth fell open. What alternate reality did these two live in?

They kept trying to soothe each other, as if they were the ones hurt by their lovers and not the other way around.

Anger swept through my body like I had never felt before. I had outbursts before and arguments, but the way the emotion enveloped me was all-encompassing. Fire filled my veins, and I knew I had to stop them. I was tired of being used and tossed aside by the people I thought cared about me, expecting me to just take it.

But right as I was about to open my mouth and tell them exactly what I thought of their pitiful life, a hand landed on my shoulder. I tilted my head, irritated that the speech I desperately wanted to shout was being delayed.

A pair of blue eyes crinkled as they gazed into mine. "Daisy. Do you want to leave this place and help my dog?"

His question was the shock of ice water in my face that I needed to melt the anger away.

I never noticed how velvety smooth Cillian's voice was until now. And then there was his smile. I wondered if I ever saw it before.

Heat was building once again, but it only pooled between my thighs.

Unable to speak, I simply nodded.

He reached for my hand and tugged me away from Andrew and Katie. I never thought Cillian Walsh would be the guy who saved me from my nightmare.

12

CILLIAN

Once we turned onto the dirt road, Daisy yelped.

It was the first sound she made since I took her away from the coffee shop earlier. Where that crazy woman I met at the vet's office two days ago, along with the man with the flowers were making it their mission to upset her.

I had gone into Hard Grind after picking up Arizona from the veterinarian clinic. The veterinarian who had fired Daisy was there. She was rude and practically threw my dog at me.

When I asked her about physical therapy services, she laughed in my face and walked away. I wasn't the only one shocked by her actions; I heard other people in the waiting room grumble about the veterinarian—and the things they said weren't pretty.

I only ran into Hard Grind to grab a quick coffee before heading home, but witnessing the look on

Daisy's face, I knew I had to step in. I understood all too well what that expression meant.

"Here we are." I glanced into the back seat once we came to a stop, where Daisy sat with Arizona.

My dog's head was in her lap as she ran her hand over his neck. I sucked in a breath at the sweet sight.

She glanced out the window, and her eyes widened. I couldn't stop drinking in her innocent wonder.

"This place is beautiful. I've never been to a farm before," she said, opening the door and hopping out.

Once I was out of the car, I stood there waiting for her to move away so I could reach in for Arizona. But Daisy beat me to it. She bent over and scooped up my dog as if he were a newborn baby.

It was insanely adorable. Tightening my jaw, I turned away. Damnit, as a hockey player, I shouldn't be oohing and ahhing over a woman with a dog. Yet I had the strongest urge to wrap them in my arms.

"Cillian, I told you Sam was taking me home." My dad strode up to my SUV.

"Hey, Dad. I decided that the farm might be a good place to work on Arizona's physical therapy."

"He's back." My dad practically pushed me aside to get closer to Arizona. "And you're going to help?" he asked Daisy with hope etched on his face.

Her large brown eyes slipped between me and my dad. "I can't since I don't work at the veterinarian clinic anymore."

My dad's head reared back. "You quit?"

I hadn't told him exactly what happened when I went back to speak with Daisy the day of the accident.

"No... but I should have." She let out a small chuckle. "I should have walked out of that place a long time ago."

"Maybe it was a good thing you got fired. Might open some doors you never would have found if you stayed," I said.

Like the one I was about to offer her.

"Fired? Who would be foolish enough to fire a talented veterinarian like you?" My dad took Arizona from Daisy, cooing at him.

"My boss is many things, and yes, foolish is definitely one of them. But, if I'm being honest, I was foolish too." Daisy frowned, wrapping her arms around herself.

"I still think this might be a gift in disguise. You're too good with animals to stay unemployed for long." I tried to bring back the smile to her face.

"Doubtful. Look where we live." She swung her arms wide. "There aren't a lot of options for me up here in the mountains. And it's not like I could start a clinic of my own. I don't have that sort of money. I live in a broom closet right now." She snorted.

"A broom closet?" Sam came up, and I noticed dirt covered the front of his jean jacket.

"It's a long story involving Szechuan chicken, an air mattress, and a selfish jerk. No, make that two selfish jerks." She sighed before she continued, "Let's just say I'm ready to start over. Maybe being a veterinarian isn't for me."

I was about to argue with Daisy when I felt something being pushed at me. My father was placing Arizona in my arms. He had a look in his eyes that told me not to question him.

"Look here, young lady," he walked over to Daisy, pointing his finger, "you saved my dog's life, and I am forever grateful for that. You have a gift, a talent. Don't throw that away just because you were fired and sleep in a broom closet."

"My dad's right, you should—"

Apparently, my father wasn't done talking as he cut me off, "Look around you. This is a farm... a farm that will have animals."

"It will?"

My dad gave me his side eye, and I knew not to ask any more questions.

"As I was saying, those animals will need a vet. Someone to help them when they're sick."

"Then you can go to the veterinarian clinic in Castle Ridge. Angelica supposedly makes house calls to farmers on Wednesdays, but I have yet to see her actually do it. Maybe she just hasn't had clients yet." Her arms slipped to her side as if she lost all energy in that moment.

"I'm not thinking about her; I'm thinking about you. Hoping someone has trained you in livestock care?" My father's lips thinned.

She took a breath and glanced around, her eyes finally settling on the red barn in the distance. "Yes, but it's been a long time. Mainly I've been dealing with cats, dogs, birds, and the occasional guinea pig. Someone brought in a goat once, but I think they kept it as a pet and not livestock."

"I see." My dad took off his worn blue baseball cap and scratched the back of his head. "Well, I happen to be getting a goat to help clear away all the weeds and excess grass. Would you look at the goat once I get it?"

Daisy nibbled her lower lip. She might be nervous, and I suspected she didn't want to disappoint my father by telling him no.

"Look, Dad, it's getting late."

He narrowed his eyes at me. "It's only three in the afternoon—"

I stepped between him and Daisy, putting my back to her, and winked at my dad. "Yes, but you know how you get if you miss the, uh... *The Golden Girls.*"

That was the first thing that popped into my head, and I could tell by my father's expression he wasn't happy with my choice in television shows.

"Right..." he said through gritted teeth. "*The Golden Girls.* Love me some Bea Arthur."

"I like *The Golden Girls* too. We can watch it together," Sam said from behind my dad.

My father leaned forward and lowered his voice. "You better know what you're doing, or it's going to be payback for this."

"I do. Now go watch your favorite show with your new *Golden Girls* buddy," I said before rolling my lips over my teeth, trying not to laugh.

My father turned and grumbled something as he walked away with Sam.

"Does he really like *The Golden Girls*?"

"No. In fact, he hates it. It was the only thing I loved to watch when I was a toddler. According to him, my mother bought the first season on videotape, and it was all I wanted to watch. He said it was on so much that he'd have trouble falling asleep at night because the theme song would seep into his head."

She frowned. "Why did you just do that? Pretend he likes *The Golden Girls* when he doen't. Why did he pretend to?"

I shifted Arizona in my arms. "Because I wanted to speak with you alone. I felt bad about you getting fired on Monday."

Daisy sighed and leaned back against the SUV. "It wasn't your fault. She had wanted me gone for a while."

That couldn't be right. Daisy was a great veterinarian; she was sweet and gentle. What veterinarian wouldn't want someone like that on their team?

"Was she jealous?"

Her brows shot up. "Jealous? Of me?" Daisy threw her head back and chuckled. "You've seen Angelica. She looks like if Salma Hayek and Sofia Vergara got together and had a baby. There's no competing with that."

"I wasn't referring to her appearance. But if that's what you meant, you're more beautiful than she could ever hope to be."

"W-What? You... you think I'm beautiful?"

Yes, but that wasn't how I planned the conversation to go.

I rubbed the back of my neck. "That's not the reason you're here."

She was so much more than breathtaking. Daisy was intelligent and playful and always brought a smile to my face—and I didn't smile very often.

She nodded and wrapped her arms around her waist. "Of course. Right."

She was unhappy. Everything coming out of my mouth was wrong, yet I couldn't stop talking. I had the strongest urge to make her smile.

"I brought you here to help Arizona. I feel like if I hadn't caused a scene with that woman and yelled at you about Arizona, your boss wouldn't have come down so hard on you. She must have found out what happened, or she wouldn't have fired you."

For the past two days, I kept going over in my head why someone would fire Daisy. Her boss must have found out how upset I was from the receptionist and assumed Daisy had something to do with it. What they didn't understand was it had nothing to do with Daisy. I was just an unreasonable asshole.

She shook her head. "Look, Cillian, it really wasn't—"

"Before you deny it and try to take the blame, I want you to know that I brought you here to offer you a job."

"What sort of job?" She gazed around the farm, taking in its charm. "Farm keep? I know about animals but not about farms, despite always wanting to live on one."

"No, not farm keep. Or farm hand. I want you to be Arizona's personal physical therapist. You can work with him here." I waved my hand around the overgrown fields.

"That's great." Her smile grew, and it felt like the sun warming my face on a chilly winter morning.

But just as her grin appeared, it slowly diminished. "But I don't have a car. How will I get here? It's not like the bus comes out this way."

"Sam and my dad. And on days they can't, I will. It's no problem."

Daisy's eyes dipped to Arizona in my arms. The dog was squirming again, so I put him down. He tried to get up to walk, but his legs wobbled before his butt fell back to the ground.

"He needs you." I pointed to my dog.

She watched Arizona as she bit her lower lip. Maybe it wasn't enough for her, just being a physical therapist. She was used to doing more.

The silence persisted, and I worried she'd say no. My brain raced to come up with more things she could do. My dad was getting a goat, so she could help the goat if it got sick. But I doubted my dad would buy a sick goat. He grew up on a farm and knew a sickly animal when he saw one.

Scratching my head, I glanced around the farm for another task.

"Okay. I'll do it," she blurted out, startling me.

"Really? That's great." I held out my hand to shake on it.

But Daisy surprised me. Her arms flew open, and she pulled me into a hug.

I hesitated for only a moment. She was soft and warm, as if her earlier smile enveloped all of me.

Folding her into my embrace, I tried not to pull her too tight. My cock had already stirred, and it wasn't good business to rub a boner all over a potential employee.

Because that was what Daisy was now, an employee. She worked for me. As my mom taught me, you should never flirt with someone you work with. I never wanted what happened to my mom with the job she had before she married my dad to happen to Daisy.

Our relationship would only ever be professional.

13

DAISY

"Right this way, Mr. Walsh," the maître d' said as he waved for us to follow.

It had been a few days since Cillian rescued me from the coffee shop and took me to his farm. Then last night I got the contract to sign to be Arizona's physical therapist. Now, he'd whisked me off to the fanciest restaurant I had ever been in.

My mouth fell open as I stared around the restaurant. I had never been to this place. Hell, I had never even heard of it.

But the thing I couldn't keep my eyes off was an enormous circular waterfall in the middle of the restaurant. The falling water glittered as it picked up the dim evening lighting from the tables.

As we made our way around it on the soft cream carpeting, I wondered about the prices I would find on the menu. I had never been to a restaurant this nice before.

"Right over here. A perfect table overlooking the mountains."

The maître d' was right. The small, white linen-covered table was set against a wall of windows that overlooked several mountains. Since it was evening, the setting sun turned the sky orange, which contrasted with the blue mountains for a breathtaking view.

The maître d' pulled out my chair, but Cillian cleared his throat. I felt my cheeks warm as I caught sight of Cillian. I wasn't used to him in a suit.

I wondered if it had been made for him. Maybe I wasn't used to seeing men in suits. Andrew never wore one; even Jackson wore a terrible white tuxedo for his wedding and looked ridiculous. I didn't tell him, but I suspected it was Katie who insisted on his wardrobe.

The light gray suit Cillian wore fit him perfectly. My eyes kept flickering to his arms. I never knew I was an arms gal, but I couldn't keep my eyes off them.

Cillian's blue eyes sparkled against the glow of the lighting as he stared down at the maître d'. The man knew well enough to step aside, allowing Cillian to hold out my chair for me. Once I was seated, I thanked him but nodded knowingly at the maître d'.

When Cillian was settled in his seat, the maître d' used his finger to press down his mustache before going over the special of the day. It was a dish I had never heard of, but the maître d' insisted it was a local delicacy. He handed us both our menus before walking away.

"I think I see Brian." Cillian turned his head.

"Isn't that the team captain?" Jackson had mentioned him a few times, but I had never met the guy.

"Yeah, but I didn't think he liked to go to places like this." Cillian shrugged and turned back to his menu.

Was Cillian the type of guy who frequented these types of restaurants? I bit down on my lower lip. He probably knew exactly which fork to use and could pronounce the menu items perfectly, even if they were in another language.

Gazing at the different dishes listed, I noticed something disturbing.

Where were the prices?

"I think I got the wrong menu," I said.

"Really?"

I turned the menu to face him. "Yes, the menu doesn't have any prices on it."

He lifted his and grinned. I sucked in a breath, as I still wasn't used to his devastating smile.

"Neither does mine. I think they purposely left the prices off the menu."

Pulling my menu back to study it, I asked, "But how do you know how much the dishes are?"

Then it hit me. You're not supposed to know the prices because if you can't afford the food, you shouldn't be dining at this restaurant.

I swallowed hard.

"Cillian, I appreciate that you wanted to take me out to dinner to thank me for helping with Arizona, but this is a little much, don't you think? I can't afford anything here. Which, I'm assuming, because I don't know the prices."

He leaned forward and placed his hand over mine. My fingers tingled from his touch.

"Daisy, I'm paying for the meal. This is me thanking you, not just for helping to get my dog walking again but for saving his life. It's the least I can do."

"But you're already paying me to work for you. And now you're paying for this expensive meal." I took a breath to get the nerve to continue. "I wanted to talk to you about how much you're paying me."

He had sent his lawyer to Lydia's place where I was still living. The lawyer had a contract for me to sign from Cillian for the work I would do for his dog. It was nice that he did things legally. When I read over the contract, that was when I saw how much he was going to pay me.

I would make more working for him than I ever did for Angelica. And while I appreciated the money, he was paying me way more than what animal physical therapists make.

I opened my mouth to explain that I made a mistake signing the contract for that amount of money when a woman appeared next to our table. She was tall with high cheekbones, and she reminded me of a runway model version of Angelica, just with strawberry blond hair.

The look in Cillian's eyes turned from warmth to ice in mere seconds.

"Cillian, I never expected to see you here again."

"Shondra. I'd say it was nice to see you again, but I'm not a liar," he said through gritted teeth.

The woman laughed, but there was a bitter tinge to it. "So funny. I'm glad you finally got your humor back. You were so depressing to be around, even when we went to Vegas. The only time you were tolerable was when you drank. Can you believe he tried to stay sober for the trip, but I talked him into partying our last night there. And what a party it was..."

He stiffened when she mentioned Las Vegas. I suspected he didn't like the memories of his time drinking.

Her green eyes shifted to me. I met her gaze, and something passed over her expression—something that raised the hairs on the back of my neck.

She smoothed her hand over her cream cashmere dress. "Oh, look. Is this another girl you're gonna whine to? Try to pull on her sympathy strings and then toss her aside the moment she doesn't want to talk about you?"

Before Cillian could respond, the woman held out her hand. "Hi, I'm Shondra, Cillian's ex-girlfriend."

Hesitantly, I took her hand. "Hello, I'm Daisy."

Her touch was icy as she gave a brisk shake before dropping my hand.

"Daisy." She tapped her chin. "That name sounds familiar, but I don't recognize you."

"Shondra, we are trying to have a nice evening, so if you would kindly fuck off—"

Shondra waved her hand at him. "Cillian, I assume you're over your mom by now." The woman rolled her eyes before focusing on me. "You just wouldn't believe the amount of whining this man did about losing his mom. I mean, I get it... your mom died. Okay. I expected some grieving for a couple of days, but then move on, am I right?"

My eyes widened as I placed my hand on my chest. I couldn't believe how callous she sounded. Shondra made Andrew seem like a decent guy.

Cillian stood. "If you don't mind getting out of our way, Shondra. We were just about to leave." He leaned forward until he was in her face with a sneer. "This place isn't what we expected. Come on, Daisy." He walked over to me and held out his hand.

I was in shock, but I understood why he wanted to go immediately. Taking his hand, I got up, and we strolled around the waterfall toward the large wooden front door.

My mouth remained closed as I clasped his hand, waiting for the car attendant to pull up with his SUV.

I glanced down at our entwined fingers, and a shiver ran up my arm. Why did something so simple like holding hands make me incredibly happy?

"You cold?" he asked.

But before I could say no, he slipped off his suit jacket and placed it over my shoulders. I tugged at the lapel, wrapping myself in his spicy scent. As much as I longed for his hand again, the jacket was nice too.

I was so out of place in that decadent restaurant, wearing my cheap, discount-store dress that I bought several years ago. When Shondra showed up, I wondered if I should have hidden under the table.

Her dress was gorgeous and hugged her body perfectly. It was made of expensive cashmere, while mine was made of polyester.

But after Shondra revealed what type of person she was, I didn't care what I looked like. Sometimes monsters were disguised in pretty packages.

The car pulled up, and Cillian handed the guy something before holding the door open for me. Once I got inside, I snuggled into his heated seats.

I waited for Cillian to speak, but the car ride home was silent. I kept wondering what I should say—something, anything to lift his spirits, but nothing felt right.

I thought about telling him how I knew what he was going through. But did I really?

I naively believed being cheated on and fired all within one week was the worst thing that could happen to someone, but that was nothing compared to someone you dearly love dying.

Cillian lost his mom, and nothing could bring her back. I could always get another job. Actually, I already had one. It wasn't something to rely on long-term and definitely not a career, but it was something to pay the bills, and helping Arizona on the farm was fun.

I was sure I'd have another boyfriend one day. Someone who wasn't a liar and a cheat.

But a mom... a mom was irreplaceable—not that I ever knew mine. But I knew what it was like to lose a parent, someone you loved dearly.

The one person he thought would care about and support him in his time of need treated him like garbage. I was starting to understand why Cillian had that chip on his shoulder.

I turned to him as we pulled up to Lydia's apartment building. I had thought about what to say. Placing my hand on his arm, I said, "I'm sorry."

He shook his head. "No, I'm sorry. I didn't realize Shondra would be there."

He wasn't getting it.

"No, Cillian. I am so sorry to hear about your mom's death."

He sat back in his car seat, letting go of the steering wheel. Weariness filled his eyes. "It was two years ago. A few months after the puke kiss."

I smirked. "That's a good name for it. Puke kiss."

There was more silence. He must still be grieving.

I reached over and grabbed his hand. Cillian flinched, but after a second, his fingers relaxed in mine. "I didn't know her, but I bet she was an amazing woman."

He nodded. "She was the type of person who found happiness in anything... even in something as terrible as cancer. When she was diagnosed with it, she said that she now had an excuse to rest and watch her soap operas."

I studied him. He stared at our hands, but his expression told me he didn't see them.

"She loved you. I may not know about the love between a mother and a son, having only ever been a daughter, but seeing the type of guy you turned out to be—"

"Yeah, a grump." He pursed his lips.

"No, I was about to say you turned out to be a nice guy. What mom wouldn't be proud at having a caring son who is also an amazing hockey player?"

His hand slipped from mine. "Hockey is just a game. I learned that the hard way after my mom died. She needed me that day, and I was too busy playing a silly game."

Oh god...

"I'm sorry. You couldn't have known she would pass that day—"

"I should have been there with her. Even the coach suggested I stay home that day to be close to her. But I chose a stick and puck over the woman I loved." He took a breath and turned toward me. "I'm sorry I couldn't take you to dinner tonight, but I need to go home."

I nodded and opened the door, stepping out. I turned back to say something before shutting the door, but it closed without me doing anything.

Heated seats and automatic closing doors? What couldn't that car do?

"Good job, Daisy. You caused another man to run away from you," I said to myself as I watched Cillian's black SUV drive away.

14

CILLIAN

"**G**ood job deflecting the puck, Aspen." I slipped on my shirt as I glanced his way.

"Thanks, Cillian. That deke you pulled on Jackson was epic." Aspen lifted his arms and danced around. Aspen was thirty, though he acted more like fifteen.

I couldn't help but laugh at his antics as I reached into my locker and pulled out my socks. Tugging them on, I noticed a few players patting Jackson on the back—one of them being Aspen. Maybe he was razzing Jackson about the deke.

Emmanuel came over and sat on the wooden bench. He bounced his foot, clearly nervous about something. Then he reached into his locker.

"Emmanuel, why is everyone congratulating Jackson?"

Since Jackson was my age, I was worried he would try to go for the captain position. I had been with the Devils longer than him and had that to my advantage, but still, I worried.

Coach hadn't mentioned anything, and Jackson hadn't formally said he was going after the position. Perhaps I was worrying about nothing.

At the moment, I was the only person up for the position, and I felt I had a good chance of getting elected. Plus, coach hadn't mentioned anything in the past week about firing me, so I might be in the clear.

"I heard Jackson was putting his hat in the ring."

"For what?"

I knew what Emmanuel meant; I just didn't want to believe it.

"He's gonna try out for team captain."

Shit. So much for being positive.

Had he heard about my date with his sister on Friday? Was it an act of retaliation?

"Jackson is throwing his hat in the ring?" My nostrils flared as I stood, turning to glare at my new competitor. "I bet it's because I want the position. He's always had it out for me."

Emmanuel said nothing, but I could tell by the look on his face that he knew something and wasn't telling me.

"Cillian, maybe it's not the right time for you to become a captain. The team is warming up to you. Focus on that." He smiled and stood, placing his hand on my shoulder. "I think you're doing a great job with that. I even heard some players talking the other day about how nice you've been lately—"

"I don't want to hear what the other players are talking about. Being captain would mean so much to…" I swallowed the lump forming in my throat. "Now I have to compete with Jackson. Everyone loves him, and he doesn't even have to try. How do I compete with that?"

Emmanuel shrugged. "He tries. Just this past Friday night, he invited the team out to a strip club—"

I turned so fast, Emmanuel stumbled back.

"I didn't hear about going to a strip club."

Emmanuel's eyebrows rose as he inched backward.

"Don't you do that, Emmanuel." I moved toward him.

He pointed behind him and raised his voice. "What's that, Aspen? Yes, of course I'll come help you get your, uh… foot out of the toilet." Emmanuel winced at his outrageous lie before turning to scurry off.

"That's right, coward, run away." Shoving my hands on my hips, I continued, "I can see Aspen over by Jackson. I'm not blind, you know."

Trying to calm down, I sucked in a few ragged breaths. "You know what? Fuck it." I ran my fingers through my hair and turned, making my way toward Jackson.

He was all smiles and laughter, entertaining a crowd of players. They noticed me first.

Their grins disintegrated as I stepped closer. Some players took a few steps back before I was directly behind Jackson.

My hand landed on his shoulder, hard. He turned and his laughter died.

"Cillian. What's up?"

"What's up?" I forced the corner of my mouth to curl. "I'll tell you what's up... I heard about the strip club."

His eyes narrowed before he glanced around the locker room. "What did you hear?"

"I heard you invited the team out to the strip club. That's funny..." I chuckled before taking a deep breath. "Because last I checked, I was part of the team too. I just don't remember being invited out."

"Why would I invite you?"

I pushed my finger in his chest and was about to answer him when he swatted my hand away.

"From what I heard, you were busy Friday night."

My nostrils flared. Daisy. She must have told him I took her to dinner.

"Jackson, I was just thanking Daisy for helping save my dog's life. That all that happened. Just dinner. Well, actually not dinner—"

"Really, Cillian? Was that all that happened? How about two years ago at a little party? Were you just thanking my sister then too when you groped her?"

He knew about that too? Daisy said she never told him. I rubbed my brow. I couldn't believe she lied to me.

I shook my head. Actually, I could believe she would lie—everyone always does. What I couldn't believe was that I fell for it.

"I've never groped your sister."

Jackson waved his hands in the air. "Groped, kissed. Same difference. That's my sister. You stay away from her."

A crowd of players had formed around us. Now everyone knew my business.

"No." The word flew out of my mouth before I had time to process what I was saying.

"No?" Jackson took a step forward, his chest bumping into mine, causing me to stumble back. "That's my sister you're talking about."

"She's an adult, Jackson. If she doesn't want to be around me, then she doesn't have to be around me. But if she does..." I licked, then bit my bottom lip.

A bunch of guys oohed, with a few snickers in the crowd.

I did not know what I was saying. It wasn't like Daisy and I were romantically involved. The two times we kissed, or almost kissed, it ended badly. She worked for me. I wasn't stupid enough to try anything with her, even if I wanted to.

Even if I thought about her every night before I went to bed and every morning when I woke up. And when I caught a whiff of the spring flowers outside, she'd pop right back into my head, no matter how hard I tried to erase her.

Despite all that, I couldn't stop myself from egging Jackson on. For years, he knew I kissed his sister, yet he said nothing. His sister and I had both dated other people since that first kiss, yet Jackson acted like I just took advantage of her. He needed to grow up, and I really itched to make him.

"So you will *not* stay away from my sister? Well... I guess I'm going to have to *make* you stay away from her then."

Before I had time to react, Jackson's fist hit my jaw. My head twisted to the side, and I felt pain explode from my jaw until it took over my entire face.

Clutching his shirt with both fists, I pushed until he slammed into the wall. Players were yelling around us, but I concentrated on Jackson's snarling face.

I reached up and grabbed his head, slamming it into the wall. As I was about to do it again, someone seized my arms, pulling me back.

I tried to shake them off, but it must have been more than one, because I couldn't get out of their hold.

"Cool it, Cillian." I heard Coach's voice in my ear.

"No one likes you, Cillian. Face it... it will be a breeze winning the captain's title," Jackson yelled as Aspen and Emmanuel held him back.

My jaw clenched. "Get off of me." I glanced back to discover both Coach and Teddy. Ugh, there was no way I was getting out of Teddy's hold.

But once I did, I'd give Jackson the lesson of his life.

"Hey, Jackson, I met your ex the other day... She told me how she wasted her time with you and wanted all this." I tried waving my hands up and down my body but couldn't, so I ended up shaking my hips.

"You fucking asshole," Jackson barked, trying to break free from Aspen and Emmanuel.

"That's it. Teddy, take Cillian to my office. I'll deal with Jackson."

As if I were as light as a sack of feathers, Teddy lifted me with one arm and carried me away. It was both humiliating and impressive.

Once we got to the coach's office, Teddy threw me inside before slamming the door to lock me in. I tried to push open the door, but he had to be standing against it.

That man was a beast.

I ran over to the windows overlooking the locker room and saw the guys dragging Jackson out. All I could do was point at him angrily. Once he was gone, I sank down onto the bench and gulped air. The anger flowing through my veins was dissolving.

Before I had time to replay the fight in my head, the door flew open, and Coach stepped inside.

"Thanks to that shit show out there, I had to send Jackson to the hospital in case he got a concussion." Coach walked right up to me and pushed his face into mine.

I didn't know what was worse, his anger or his breath.

I stood, causing him to back up. "He fucking started it."

"You sound like a five-year-old, Cillian. My kids are better behaved than you two are. If this is about the captain position, then you both can consider yourself out of the running."

My eyes widened. "You can't do that, Coach. It's up to the team—"

"I'm part of the team. In fact, I'm head of the team. And if I tell the team they can't vote for you, then they won't."

I ran my fingers through my hair and took a few steps around his office. "I'm sorry." I let out a breath. "It wasn't about the captain position; it was about his sister, Daisy."

"Really? What does Daisy have to do with this?" Before I could respond, he shook his head. "Cillian, did you have sex with his sister at that party you told me about?"

"No, I swear. But Jackson thinks I groped her or did something to her, and he's angry."

"Then you explain nothing happened and move on."

"I tried, but he keeps telling me to stay away from her."

Coach shrugged. "Then do that. It's not like you run in the same circles. Do you?"

"Technically, no, but I can't stay away from her."

Coach walked over to his desk and sat in his chair. "And why can't you stay away from her?"

I guessed I could; I didn't have to be at the physical therapy appointments. Besides, my dad would be at the farm. I was sure if I asked Sam to pick her up and take her home, he'd do it.

If I worked it right, I'd never have to see Daisy again.

"Because I don't want to stay away from her."

15

DAISY

I glanced down at my phone in confusion.

Stay away from Cillian. That's an order.

I texted my brother back.

We r not in the military and you r not my superior.

I shook my head and put my phone back in my pocket. I guess Cillian upset him at practice today.

My phone vibrated in my pants pocket, but I ignored it. My brother was just being a protective jerk. He had always been that way with me—even when I first started dating Andrew.

Our relationship was simple—he tried his best to keep me away from guys, and I helped clean up his messes. Our father died when we were young. I had just turned thirteen, and he was twenty. Our mom had never been in the picture. He tried reaching out to her once Dad died, but then told me he couldn't find her.

We were both too young to take over parenting each other, yet that was exactly what we did. I was less like a sister and more like a mother taking care of his problems. He was less like a brother and more like a protective father.

Now that I thought about it, perhaps I shouldn't have stopped my brother from scaring off Andrew. It would have saved me heartache and losing a job.

I had spent most of the morning working with Arizona on the farm. Sam and Mr. Walsh picked me up this morning at my apartment building.

By lunchtime, I suspected I wore Arizona out. I let him rest in the empty barn, and Mr. Walsh gave him a bone he had brought with him. I ended up helping the guys clear the field.

While Mr. Walsh told me I didn't have to help on the farm, it wouldn't be right for me to sit around while they did all the hard work. With what Cillian was paying me, I felt uneasy doing only a few hours of work with Arizona. I wasn't about to take advantage of his kindness.

I wiped the sweat from my brow and straightened my back. It was a cool spring day, and I had taken off my jacket an hour ago because of the physical labor.

The sun was in my eyes as I gazed toward the farmhouse. Someone was walking toward me—probably Sam letting me know he was ready to leave. I leaned the rake against the wooden fence and removed the work gloves Mr. Walsh let me borrow.

"Why did you lie to me?" he called out.

My head jerked back. Why would Sam think I lied to him?

"About what? If you're asking about Arizona, I can't—"

There was a moment of clarity as his head blocked the sun, and I saw who was coming toward me. Cillian eyes bore into me, and he didn't appear happy.

"Cillian? Why are you here? Sam is going to take me home."

"They left."

My heart hit the ground, and for a moment, I wondered how I would get home.

He walked up and stood there in nothing but a T-shirt and jeans. It surprised me that he didn't have a jacket on—it wasn't like he was doing farm work. But the more I stared at the Devils T-shirt, the more I became fascinated with how it clung to his chest. Either he put it on straight out of the shower, or he was dripping in sweat.

"But they were my ride home."

He folded his arms over his chest, emphasizing his muscles. *Look at those arms.* I'd be happy to binge watch the hell out of them. There was no doubt about it, the man was built. I wondered what it would be like to trace my finger over the curves in his arms and chest... and possibly even lower.

I cleared my throat, trying to distract myself from his glistening arms.

"You never answered my question. Why did you lie to me?"

I gave him a perplexed look, unsure what he was asking. "About what?"

He laughed, and I sucked in a breath. Cillian was achingly beautiful when humor touched his features.

"You said you never told your brother about us... about the kissing. And then he found out about the date we had on Friday."

"I swear, I never told him."

He shook his head. "It doesn't matter. Anytime I get close to you, you make up some excuse why you don't want me near you."

"Is this about the kiss? I react badly to alcohol—"

He waved his hand in the air. "Yes, I already heard that one. But what about your birthday party in the closet over a week ago? You acted as if you couldn't wait to get out of there. When your friend finally let you out, you said you were glad they showed up. Then, you left me in the closet."

I replayed the moment in my head. "No, that's not what happened."

He took a step forward until I felt his body heat, and his warmth caused my heart to beat a little faster.

"I was there too. I think I remember what we did before that closet door opened and after."

I rubbed my face. Now that I thought about it, I realized what he said was true.

True for him.

"I'm sorry. I didn't mean I was glad to be rescued from *you*. It was the stuffy closet. I was glad to be out of that tiny room. I went off to get us some water, and when I returned, you were already gone."

His gaze scanned my face until it landed on my lips. The intensity of his stare sent a shiver down my spine.

"And you didn't tell your brother?"

I rolled my eyes. "I am guessing you don't have siblings."

He shook his head.

"The last person I would tell about who I kissed would be my brother."

Cillian took another step toward me, causing me to move backward until my back hit the wooden fence. The top rail dug into my spine.

He was so close I had to tilt my head up to gaze into his darkening blue eyes. Cillian's hot breath drifted over my cheeks and down my neck. Instinctively, my hands lifted, pressing against his chest. His eyes flashed with heat as he licked his lips, and for a moment, I forgot what we were discussing.

"Then how did he find out about *us*?" He emphasized the last word as if it was a declaration. That one word had so much meaning.

"Us?" I whispered, unable to tear my eyes from his lips.

He grabbed the wood railing on either side of me, pinning me in place. Cillian leaned forward, only stopping once his lips brushed against my ear. "Us, Daisy. You and me. My lips on you."

I nodded, only wanting to do what he suggested. "I'd like that," I said as my fingers clasped behind his neck.

The corner of his lips curled, and it was sinister. Swallowing, I felt more like prey than a woman doing farm work.

"There's no one here. I could do a lot more than kiss you... If you'd like?"

What was happening? One moment Cillian was calling me a liar, and the next, he was pushing his body against mine. And I was pretty sure it wasn't a banana in his pants pocket that was rubbing against my stomach.

"I'd like..." Words were not my strong suit at the moment. I closed my eyes, half out of embarrassment and half out of the hope he understood what I meant.

He did. His lips were there, firmly crashing onto mine.

My mouth opened, letting a moan escape, but Cillian took it as a chance to plunder. His tongue danced with mine. His arms wrapped around me, pulling me tight, and I was totally sure there was no fruit in his pockets... it was all cock.

My leg slid around his as I tried, unsuccessfully, to climb his body. He knew what I was attempting as his hands slid down my back until they cupped my ass.

I gasped as he lifted me, setting me back on top of the railing. That was better. Now I could wrap both my legs around him, and I was level with him.

Cillian broke our kiss. His eyes were wild with hints of uncertainty. "This isn't right..."

No. Don't do this. Don't run away.

"How can this not be right? Because of my brother? This isn't the eighteen hundreds, and he's not my keeper."

Cillian shook his head. "Not your brother. I meant you and me. You work for me."

I tilted my head. "And? It's not like it's a law that people who work together can't, you know... do what we're doing." My cheeks warmed at the thought of where this was going. A make-out session against a fence seemed rather harmless, yet I knew my nipples were hardening by imagining what we could do together.

"Yes, but—"

I cut him off with another kiss, and he didn't resist. I knew I made the right decision when his hand snaked up my side, sliding under my shirt and cupping my breast.

His thumb grazed my nipple, and my back arched. I moaned and threw my head back. Cillian didn't stop his kiss; instead, he moved down my neck until he hit my chest.

This felt so right. I hoped he didn't have another change of heart.

I reached down and lifted my shirt just in case the fabric in the way made him change his mind about the kissing.

"Daisy... do you want me to stop?" he asked with a growl.

"It seems to me that I'm helping you do it, so no, I really don't want you to stop."

His finger slid along the edge of my lace bra before tugging it down. My nipple popped out, the cold air turning it to a spike.

Cillian leaned forward and captured my nipple with his lips as electricity shot straight down to my core. I reached around his head, running my fingers through his soft waves.

Before long, he leaned over and did the same to my other nipple. I was so wet. The thoughts running through my head of what I wanted to do to him were becoming dirtier by the second.

I took his hand off my chest and moved it down my body. He understood at once what I wanted. Maybe it was what I had dealt with the past few weeks, but I needed relief. I desired an orgasm, and I wanted Cillian to give it to me.

His fingers undid my jeans—with some help from me—and slid under my panties. The moment his finger brushed my clit, I gasped.

Cillian looked up, his eyes ablaze with heat. "We're doing this."

I didn't know what he meant, but I was up for anything he wanted to do. Unfortunately, what he wanted required his hand to leave my core.

"What's happening—" I asked before he wrapped his arms around me and took me off the fence, placing me back on the ground.

"Take off your jeans and your underwear," he demanded with hooded eyes.

I had never witnessed anything sexier in my life. Fumbling with my jeans, I pulled until they were a heap in the grass. Shortly after, my panties joined them.

Cillian glanced at my pile of clothes before looking up at me. "We're about to fuck, Daisy. But first, I want to taste you."

Correction, *that* was the sexiest thing I had ever heard in my life.

He lowered onto his knees and told me to lean back against the fence. Once I did, he took my leg and hooked it over his shoulder. I bit my lip in anticipation, my body vibrating at the thought of what he would do to me.

Lowering his head, I gripped the railing the moment his tongue swiped my clit. Cillian moaned right before he said, "Damn, you taste so good."

Fuck. I would not last very long. Had Andrew ever been this good? No. Cillian had barely done anything to me, and already, he was better than Andrew at sex.

He slipped his fingers into my core as his lips and tongue danced with my clit. I fisted Cillian's hair, hoping I wasn't hurting him, but I was too far gone to control what my extremities were doing.

"Oh, God, I'm coming," I warned Cillian, closing my eyes.

His tongue didn't quit drawing out my orgasm.

Time had passed, but I couldn't tell how much when I finally came back to earth.

When I opened my eyes, I got a happy surprise. Cillian had his jeans pulled down and a large, hard cock in his hand. He was stroking it and gazing at me as if I were his main meal.

16

CILLIAN

Her pussy was so good, I was almost disappointed when she came. *Almost.* But it was worth it when I heard my name on her lips, crying out in delight.

I checked my wallet, and by some miracle, I had a condom in there. Once I had rolled it on my aching cock, even the cool breeze couldn't dull the fire that burned inside me for Daisy's pussy.

She glanced around. "How do you want to do this...? Should I lie in the grass?" Daisy frowned as she stared at the dead weeds by her feet.

I reached forward, cupping her chin. "I'd never make you lie on dirt."

An adorable wrinkle formed between her brows. She didn't understand what I was planning to do, so I showed her instead.

Wrapping my arms around her, I clutched her firm ass with both hands. She gasped as I lifted her.

"What are you—" Her words melted into a moan as I impaled her on my cock.

"Does this answer your question?" I pressed her against the fence, and my hips shifted into her.

Her head fell back, and it was as if her milky neck beckoned me to lap her up. I loved listening to her tiny whimpers as I dotted kisses up to her ear.

Daisy's fingernails clawed at my upper arms. There was something about how she clung to me that drove me wild.

I never had that with my ex. It always seemed like Shondra was acting, like she was in a porno and had to be overly sexual while we fucked. But with Daisy, the way she reacted to my touch, to my cock, was natural. Like she couldn't get enough of me, and because of that, I never wanted this to end.

"God, I love your arms," she said with a groan.

I licked my lips as I watched her study my body. "Good to know. I'll make sure they hold you close any chance I get. Would you like that?"

Her hips ground down on me, and I had my answer.

"Fuck, you're so tight," I said, trying to hold back my release.

The way she met every thrust and shifted her hips, I knew it wouldn't be long until I exploded. Lifting and setting her on the railing, I moved my hand until it was between us. My thumb reached down to rub her clit.

Daisy hissed, but from the way she moved her body, I knew she wanted more.

It wasn't long before I felt her tighten around my cock. Next time I'd make this last. We'd do it on a bed, perhaps after a delightful meal, while I took my time tasting her. Not against an old wooden fence where we were working hard to get each other off.

"Cillian!"

I watched her whither in my arms as her climax took hold.

There was no holding back. I came, pressing my face against her neck. My body shuddered with euphoria as I pushed into her. She was soft and warm, and I never wanted to let her go.

As the ripples of pleasure slowly faded, I lifted my head, brushing a kiss on her chin.

"Thanks. I needed that." Daisy's flushed cheeks wrinkled as she smiled. I wanted every expression, every line and wrinkle imprinted in my memory forever.

"I'm glad I could give you what you needed." I couldn't stop peppering kisses on her cheek and down her neck.

A shiver ran down her body.

Straightening, I asked, "Are you cold?"

Without waiting for her answer, I took a step back and lowered her to the ground. Her legs wobbled, so I held my arm around her until she found her footing.

"Two orgasms in one go. I think that's a record," she said with a laugh, searching the ground for her clothes.

I tilted my head. "You've never had more than two orgasms with sex? I know it's usually only one with guys, but multiple orgasms aren't unusual for women."

She pulled up her jeans and focused on buttoning her fly. "Huh. Well, it's never happened to me. Andrew was never the attentive lover. You know, the guy with the bouquet who was in the coffee shop the other day. I think he cared more about his pleasure than mine."

I folded my arms. That pissed me off. The more I learned about her ex, the more it dumbfounded me that a guy could be that stupid. He had a hard-working, beautiful woman, and he treated her like garbage.

"I guess you're glad you're not with him anymore. Sounds like a dud to me." I was doing my best to be polite.

She took a deep breath and rubbed her arms after adjusting her shirt. "I'm realizing that more and more each day. It was like Angelica did me a favor by sleeping with him."

My eyes widened. "You're telling me your boss slept with Andrew?" All the pieces were falling together in my head. "Then she fired you."

Daisy nodded. "Yup. Now you can see you weren't responsible for me losing my job. She wanted me gone because I was a reminder about what a terrible thing she did. But now that I think about it, she really didn't care about my feelings at all."

I wrapped my arms around Daisy, trying to keep her warm. "She seems like the type of person who doesn't care about anyone's feelings."

Daisy smiled, her hand lying on my chest. "You're a much better boss."

I stiffened. "About that. Uh…"

"Don't tell me you're about to fire me too?" She chuckled, but her smile slowly faded when I didn't answer. She took a step back and let my arm fall away. "Cillian… are you serious? You have sex with me, and then I'm done? No more Daisy?"

I shook my head. "No, that's not it at all. I just don't feel comfortable with you working for me and us having sex. I don't want you to feel like you have to do this in order to keep the job."

My mom told me once that she had a job right before my dad proposed to her. The boss at the job propositioned her and told her that if she wanted to keep working there, she'd have to sleep with him. My dad found out, and apparently, the next day, the boss had a black eye. Then my mom quit and helped my dad on the farm.

It never sat well with me about what happened to her, and I would never want to put Daisy in that position.

Her brows pinched together. "So, if I had said no to you at any time, you wouldn't have stopped?"

"No. I would have backed off immediately. Like I said, I don't want you to feel that you have to have sex with me, you know… to keep the job."

She put her hands on her hips. "Cillian, I was practically ripping my clothes off and guiding you. There was nothing about this that made me feel uncomfortable, except maybe the few splinters I have in my ass from the fence."

"Are you sure you're fine working for me?"

She shrugged as a grin tugged at the corner of her mouth. "I'm working with your dog. The only reason I see you is if my brother has upset you."

I took a step closer and placed my hands on her hips. "Can I see you even if your brother hasn't irritated me?"

Daisy nodded, her finger drawing circles on my arm. "I'm hoping there are many reasons you'd want to see me. Like if you want to take a walk or grab a slice of pizza or—"

My cock was stirring again.

"When you talk about pizza, there's no holding me back. It's almost like you want to get more splinters in your ass." I nibbled on her neck.

Her body rumbled with laughter, and I knew there was no better feeling than holding Daisy in my arms.

17

DAISY

"**M**eet Lucky," my nephew said as he tried to pick up the puppy from the gray carpeted floor.

I shrugged off my coat and hung it up in Jackson's small coat closet. I had spent the morning working at Cillian's farm with Arizona and then the evening helping at Big Mountain Animal Rescue. Saying I was exhausted would be an understatement, but I always made time for my nephew.

I had been fooling around with Cillian for five days. Thoughts of us meeting up at the farm after his father and Sam left for the day caused my cheeks to warm. But today I just didn't have the time.

Despite our secrecy, I worried it would get back to my brother.

However, he found out about our kissing, and I wondered if that was how he would discover our relationship. If he was going to find out, I wanted it to be from me.

Knowing he didn't have a game tonight, I called my brother and offered to bring over pizza. He never turned down free food, but his tone had me worried that he already knew about Cillian.

I smiled at my nephew and then gnawed on my lower lip, wondering if I should mention that I had already met the dog or not. It might add another nail in my coffin with my brother.

I decided on the latter.

"What a cutie." I lowered myself onto my haunches as the puppy ran over to lick my face. "I'm watching a cat named Fierce. Well, actually, my roommate Sophia seems to be taking care of her a lot. I think she's taken to the cat, which is a surprise since I never thought of her as an animal lover."

The look on Lucas's face told me he didn't care at all about my roommate and only had eyes for his new puppy. "Where did Lucky come from?"

"Mommy gave him to me." Lucas wrapped his arms around the dog, trying for a hug, but Lucky was having none of it.

"That's so great." I stood.

"Yes, wonderful. A surprise pet. Who doesn't love that? It's like we live in a Hallmark movie." Jackson's words came out laced with bitterness.

He stood in the kitchen archway with folded arms after placing the pizza on the counter. Worry lines etched his features. He seemed even more unhappy than usual. I knew he wouldn't be as excited about the puppy as his son, but the way he looked, I was nervous he was mad about my relationship with Cillian.

"I'm here to help. If you need dog food or some quick medical help, I'm your gal," I said, trying to cheer my brother up and get on his good side.

He rubbed his face and nodded. "Thanks, Sis. You don't have to do all that. Katie mentioned you were no longer working at the veterinarian clinic."

I sighed and walked over to the couch. Maybe he didn't know about us yet. I sat down, intending to peel off the bandage and just blurt out that I was dating Cillian. Each day Cillian and I were together, the paranoia of my brother discovering us became worse. But sitting on his uncomfortable couch, my cowardliness increased.

My brother pushed off the doorway and came over to the couch. I bounced a little as he sat next to me.

"It's fine. Angelica fired me."

"What? After what she did to you, she turned around and fired you?" He sat back with a sigh. "She's stupid. She hung on to that loser ex of yours and fired the only competent vet at her clinic. Watch, within the week, she's going to be begging you back."

I shrugged. "It would be too late then. Because I got a job, and it pays better than what I was making at the clinic."

"Really? Wait, you aren't working at The Blue Spot? You're too good with animals to be catering to spoiled rich people."

My brother and I had the same opinion about that fancy resort and all the people in it.

"No, I'm not working at The Blue Spot. The reason I brought the pizza over tonight for us was because I wanted to talk to you about my new boss."

"Okay, great." His eyes widened. "Wait, are you going to be working for the Devils? Like in administration or something like that? Daisy, that would be so great. I'm so happy for you—"

I held up my hands, stopping him. "No, I'm not working for the Devils."

He appeared even more confused than before. "Then who is it? And why would you need to discuss this with me in person?"

I took a deep breath to garner the courage to let my brother know I was working for his enemy. He wasn't good at handling me doing things he didn't like. I loved my brother, but he had trouble accepting that I was an adult and could make my own decisions.

It also didn't help with Katie dropping the puppy on him. I knew she wouldn't be any help. My brother had that look on his face when I arrived that told me Katie was making trouble once again.

"My new boss is Cillian."

There was silence, and my brother's smile fell so fast, I thought it might shatter.

"You mean Cillian Walsh, the Grumpy Old Man of hockey?"

"Yes, Jackson," I groaned. "But Cillian isn't the bad guy you think he is. I have—"

He didn't wait for me to finish. "Wait a second..." Jackson shifted on the couch toward me. "Daisy, does this have to do with that kiss you two shared two years ago?"

"No, it doesn't. I'm working for him because he was there when I got fired. I was helping his dog, and that's when Angelica came in. She didn't like how I handled the situation, so she fired me right in front of Cillian."

"Cillian got you fired? And now you want to work for him?"

Ugh. I knew he'd twist it to blame Cillian.

"Jackson, that's not what happened. Cillian did nothing to get me fired."

Jackson folded his arms over his chest. "So, he didn't complain about your qualifications or that you weren't doing a good enough job? Because if I know him, those would be the first things out of his mouth."

I pursed my lips. Cillian had complained about everything Jackson was saying, but I didn't want to tell my brother that. "It's not why I was fired. Angelica wanted me gone; you know that."

"Did she though? Because, as you know, you're a better veterinarian than she is. Everyone in town knows that. Why would she want to get rid of the person who was basically keeping her clinic open?"

My cheeks warmed. I appreciated what my brother was saying, but I didn't believe what he said was totally true. "It's her clinic, Jackson. If she was that bad, people wouldn't take their pets there."

"They went there because of you. Even Katie complained about Angelica."

I shook my head. "I still think she wanted to fire me because of the Andrew situation, and she saw Cillian's dog situation as the perfect excuse. You weren't there, Jackson."

"I don't have to be there. I know Cillian, and I know how bad your boss is." He leaned over and took my hand in his. "If she wanted you fired, she would have had plenty of time to do it before then. You've got to ask yourself, why did she choose that moment to fire you? It was because of Cillian. She must have heard him complain, or at the very least, word got back to her about what a jerk he was about everything." He took a breath before he let my hand go. "But... Maybe I'm just bent out of shape because of seeing Katie again. I'm glad he's attempting to make up for getting you fired by offering you a job. What exactly are you doing for him?"

"I'm helping his dog walk again after his leg was amputated. Just physical therapy, but I get to do it on a farm. His father owns a farm, and he's busy fixing it up, so I'm there every day with his father helping Cillian's dog learn to walk again."

My brother nodded, satisfied by my answer. "I'm happy you got a job, but I still don't trust Cillian. He'll screw you over somehow; he always does."

Jackson got up and went over to play with his son and the new puppy. I sat there watching them. Despite my brother's hardships, love surrounded him. He never let it affect how he treated others.

I couldn't say the same for Cillian. Maybe Jackson was right? Could Cillian have played a hand in getting me fired?

I didn't think he meant to do it, and he had made up for it by offering me the job of helping his dog. With a frown, I realized the job offer was out of pity. Jackson thought Cillian was going to screw me over, and he wouldn't be the first guy to do that to me.

Shaking myself out of the negative thoughts, I smiled at my nephew. I knew Jackson didn't like Cillian. He didn't want me working for his teammate, and he got it in his head that it was all his fault.

Angelica had wanted me gone, and the dog surgery was the reason she used to get rid of me.

That was it. At least, I hoped.

18

CILLIAN

My lips brushed Daisy's cheek. She was soft as a petal.

"It's getting late... Don't you have a game tomorrow? I thought players didn't have sex before games."

I chuckled, lifting myself on my arm. We had been having sex at the farm, and the only soft surface was an old couch in the living room. It was rather thin, so I had to lie on my side or Daisy would fall off.

I had wanted to bring her to my bed at home, but she felt it was best to keep our relationship a secret. I understood to a point—her brother would go ballistic and would do everything in his power to destroy my chances at team captain.

I shouldn't lust after my teammate's sister. But my black heart seemed to lighten when she was around.

But even after the vote next week, she wanted to wait to tell people about us.

I watched her nipple harden as my finger circled around it. "Where did you hear that?"

She twisted her head, that adorable wrinkle between her brows appearing. I moved my finger up to trace that tiny line.

"I don't know. I thought it was just a thing. That players needed all their strength."

I didn't like pretending around the guys on the team, and especially my dad. Daisy made my heart soar, and as corny as it sounded, I wanted to tell everyone. But it was what Daisy wanted, and so I bit my tongue, even around Jackson.

Which wasn't easy because he was being even more of a dick than usual. A part of me wanted to taunt him with the fact that I was seeing his sister, knowing he'd blow up.

"I'll have plenty of strength."

God, Daisy was beautiful. The sun was setting, and an orange band of light filtered in, hitting her hair just right. It sparkled with flecks of gold mixed with her brown hair. She shimmered like a goddess.

"I guess that means no sex tomorrow." She frowned, but the way her hand slid down my side and wrapped around my cock told me she wasn't too unhappy to fool around some more.

"I don't see why not. Just come to the game. You can come back to my place after, and we can have sex in a real bed. We can order pizza and make a night of it."

That would be perfect. Celebrating with pizza, because there was no way we'd lose to Sacramento. They were the worst team in the league.

Then after, she'd sleep over, keeping me warm. And I'd make sure to keep Daisy awake with pleasure all night long.

She turned her head, staring out the window. "You know I can't."

I took a deep breath. Shondra used to say the same thing to me—make up excuses as to why she couldn't come see me play. I realized later it was because she didn't care about me; she only cared about my money.

"I don't see why not." I pulled her hand away from my dick and sat up.

It was time things began to change between us. My heart ached for Daisy. As much as I understood why we had to wait to tell others about our relationship, it was starting to feel strange going out of our way to ignore one another.

Daisy sat up, pulling the soft blanket I brought over around her shoulders. "What happens when I'm at the game? Everyone's gonna assume I'm there to cheer on my brother. But what if I cheer you on? People are going to notice."

I stared at her with my mouth wide open. My heart pounded as a thought bubbled to the surface. "Are you embarrassed to be with me?"

Daisy shook her head, pain in her eyes. "No, not at all. I really like being with you, Cillian. But Jackson is going through a tough time right now, and I want to ease him into it with us."

"Then the perfect way to ease him into it is if you start coming to our games, and then he'll see you around me a bit."

I was hoping she'd be more open to it the more I talked about it. If taking it slow was what Daisy wanted, I'd work to make it happen. If she wanted me to kiss Jackson's ass, I'd do it.

Daisy shook her head. "It's not the right time. Jackson is—"

I stood and put my hands on my hips. Her eyes flew to my cock, and I couldn't help but enjoy the way she looked at me. "Our relationship shouldn't be dependent on Jackson. He's already going to beat me and become team captain. I feel like I'm losing everything to that guy."

Daisy stood and wrapped her arms around me, covering the both of us in the blanket. "I didn't realize you two were up for team captain. Congratulations, Cillian. Why do you think Jackson is going to win?"

"Because everyone loves Jackson. I've been working hard to not be so grumpy with the players." Daisy giggled, but I continued, "But once I found out I was up against him, I knew everyone would vote for him."

She sighed. "I love my brother, but he's not the leader type. He's a great hockey player, will always be there for me and the people he cares about, but if

I had to choose between you both for team captain, I'd choose you."

Daisy nibbled on her lower lip. "Maybe I shouldn't do this, but if you want, I can help you if you need it. I don't know what I could do to help, but whatever you want, I'll get it for you."

I smiled. "Really? You'll help me?"

She nodded. "Yes, I care about you. I want you to succeed. You helped me when I needed it, and it's the least I can do."

Was she doing this because she felt obligated to pay me back? I gave my head a little shake. No, I wasn't going to let those negative thoughts inside my head. Daisy was a sweet woman; she wasn't Shondra.

"You can help me come up with some ideas for an event to do with the players. I want to show the coach that I can come up with interesting charity events like a captain would. But at the same time, something the guys would like. Jackson took them to the strip club, and that pretty much cemented their vote for him, but that's not an event a team captain would arrange. I want to do something that shows my skills while also making the team happy."

It was right then that Arizona hobbled into the room. Daisy had done a great job helping him learn to walk, and he could now go short distances. Our walks outside didn't last long, but it was better than I could have ever imagined. Daisy believed with a few more weeks of therapy, he would be hopping around like his old self.

Daisy glanced over at Arizona and smiled. "You want an event? Something the team would enjoy?" She scratched at her chin.

"Yeah, I could take them out to a nice restaurant, but I don't know if a lot of the players would be into that."

"I have an idea, Cillian. How about an adopt-a-thon?"

"What?"

She took a step back and waved toward the window. "I volunteer at Big Mountain Animal Rescue. They want to have an adoption event but are having trouble finding a space. Normally I would let them use the veterinarian clinic, but since I no longer work there, they can't use that place. They've been scrambling trying to find a location to hold it. How about the farm? This would be the perfect location to hold it. There's lots of room."

I stared out the window and mulled over her words. Glancing down at the smartest woman I knew, I couldn't stop the grin that grew on my face. "That's a great idea, Daisy. Who doesn't like animals? The guys are going to love it."

At least, I hoped they would. Did it really compare to strippers? Not really, but I bet the coach would love it. At the very least, I'd stay on the team. I couldn't see the coach firing me after doing an adopt-a-thon.

Daisy was incredibly excited. What she didn't realize was that Jackson was going to start to ask questions.

161

He'd wonder why I was holding an adopt-a-thon with Daisy. I just hoped Daisy didn't realize that, or she wouldn't want to help me.

Any chance to be close to Daisy, I'd take it.

19

DAISY

"**A**re you sure about this?" Lydia asked as she held my hand.

We stood in front of the white painted door. The April air was warming, and a shiver ran down my arm at what I was about to do.

The past several days had been hectic.

I had spent all my time helping fix up the farm to host the adopt-a-thon event. When I told Big Mountain Animal Rescue about the location, they were overjoyed. Even Harper and Sophia helped hand out flyers to all the local businesses about the event. Lydia had a family emergency and couldn't help.

Doing all that work had me exhausted. Cillian and I hadn't even had a chance to be alone together. He was always at practice or a game or helping on the farm, but when I wasn't there. He told me the entire team wanted to help with the animals.

"I have to. It's time. No offense, but that broom closet doesn't make a great bedroom."

Lydia shrugged. "I never thought it would. It was your idea."

"Why didn't you talk me out of it?" I almost wish I could magically travel back in time to slap myself for even mentioning the closet.

Lydia placed her hand on my shoulder and turned to face me. "Daisy, I love you, but you were going through a rough time. I wasn't about to tell you no, you couldn't sleep at my home. If you wanted it to be the closet, I wasn't about to talk you out of it."

I nodded. She was right. I was lost then. My heart was broken, and I couldn't see straight. Maybe I needed to experience sleeping in that tiny space to open my eyes to what was right in front of me. Cillian.

I bit my lower lip just thinking about him. The things he did to my body... no man had ever done to me. It was killing me that I couldn't be with him this week.

"You've got that look," Lydia said as she smiled.

"What look?"

"The I've-been-fucked-good look. You only had that once before with that guy in college... the football player. What was his name?"

"Dawyne."

Dawyne was the guy who gave me my first orgasm with sex. He took the time to explore my body, and he did a great job of it. Very thorough.

"I never had this look with Andrew?"

Lydia's eyes shot up. "Oh, no. Not once."

"Then why was I with him?" I murmured more to myself than to her.

"I asked myself the same question. He was your boyfriend, and I figured you saw something in him I didn't."

I scratched my head, trying to remember if there was a moment where Andrew had won me over. There was nothing. He was nice enough to me. Paid me a compliment now and then for the first year. When we moved in together, he turned more into a roommate than a boyfriend.

"I don't know." I must have had a sad look on my face because Lydia rubbed my back—something she only did when I was feeling down.

"It doesn't matter now because it's obvious there's someone else. Who is it? One of Jackson's teammates? Those hockey players are super hot. Except for that Emmanuel guy." She rolled her eyes.

"What's wrong with him?"

"Nothing." She shook her head. "Just some drunken antics at your birthday party. I didn't like what he said. Don't worry about it; he was probably just drunk."

There was something she wasn't telling me.

"Okay. You guessed it. There is something going on with a hockey player, but not Emmanuel. I just can't really tell you right now."

She gasped and placed her hand on her chest. "I've been your best friend since fifth grade, and this is what you do?"

"It's not like that. The only reason I am keeping it a secret is because I don't want Jackson to find out."

"He's going to find out at some point, anyway."

"Just not right now. Why is this so hard to understand? Even, uh... the guy I'm dating wants it out in the open."

"Good for him. At least he's proud to be by your side. I get you want to protect Jackson, but you are his little sister, not his big sister. He can take care of himself. Sometimes I think you coddle him too much."

My head shot back. "What? How do I coddle my brother?"

"I like Jackson, but he needs to figure things out for himself. He gets his heart broken by his shitty ex-wife, and you run over and take over as a parent to his child."

I folded my arms over my chest. "I'm his aunt and would do anything for Lucas."

"Yes, you buy your nephew anything he needs and happen to always stop by the grocery store to pick up a few things whenever you head over to your brother's place. I understand he has money troubles, but this happened long before Katie."

I didn't like where the conversation was heading. "I'm just a loving sister."

"You are, Daisy. I'd love to have you as my sibling instead of being stuck with my brother. Even my grandmother told me she's leaving the house to me instead of Frasier because she thought he wasn't wise with money. Her words, not mine."

"I don't want Jackson to have money problems. I know I'm a little overprotective, but it's because I love him."

She took a step forward and pulled me into a hug. "I love that you have a big heart. I just wish someone would do something for you for once, instead of you doing everything for everyone else."

Perhaps that was why I ended up with Andrew. I took the idea of taking care of the people I love way too far; I went overboard. And because I helped them so much, I attracted guys who took advantage of that, like Andrew.

Was Cillian like that? He had a job, a well-paying one. And he had a home. He took care of his dad and would do anything for his dog.

Nope. Cillian wasn't like that at all.

"Enough of my therapy session." I winked. "It's time to move back into my apartment."

I took my keys out of my pocket and moved them toward the door handle. But right as I was about to push them in the keyhole, the door flew open.

Andrew stood on the other side of the door in my terrycloth robe—which really didn't fit him—a stained white T-shirt, and a pair of blue plaid pajama pants.

"I thought I heard voices out here." He had a grin on his face that was accentuated by either red lipstick or pasta sauce.

Based on the smell from the apartment, I suspected it was sauce on his face.

"Andrew... You're here," Lydia said with surprise.

He tilted his head and chuckled. "Why wouldn't I be here? I live here."

"But I pay the rent," I said.

He took a step out, and that was when I noticed he was wearing my slippers too, crushing the heel. Andrew threw an arm around me. "I know. You're the best girlfriend a guy could ask for."

"Girlfriend?" Lydia and I said at the same time.

"You both are hilarious. Come inside. No need for you two to be standing out in the cold."

He directed me inside, and, in my confusion, I followed.

"Oh, my god..." Lydia mumbled.

I assumed she was reacting to the wreckage that was my apartment. It looked like a university frat party competition was held in my apartment, where fraternities had to outdo each other with filth and odor.

There were beer cans, pizza boxes, and dirty dishes piled on every surface. There was even a dirty glass in the eucalyptus pot by the window.

"What happened?" I asked.

Something must have occurred. Maybe he had a party last night and hadn't cleaned up yet. There was no way one man could have made a mess like that in just a few weeks.

"Nothing happened. You weren't here to clean so..." He waved his hand around the room.

I shoved my hands on my hips. "Why didn't *you* clean up? This is your mess."

His shoulders sank, and I swear, it looked like Andrew was about to throw a tantrum.

"You know I hate cleaning, Daisy. That's just me. I've done a lot of thinking while you haven't been here, and I realized you never accepted me for who I am. I need to have someone clean up after me, someone to take care of me. I don't think I'm meant to work."

My eyes widened. "I guess you're lucky you got Angelica."

If Angelica were here, I'd be down on my knees thanking her for saving me from the spoiled man-child who stood in front of me.

He rubbed his face, smearing the sauce over his nose. "We ended things." He let out a breath. "I was hoping to move in with her, but she said no. And then, once she found out I didn't intend to get a job, she left me. She's having trouble with the clinic. She doesn't have many clients left."

My brow rose at what he said about the clinic.

"What happened to her clients?" Lydia asked as if reading my mind.

He shrugged. "She mentioned a few of them complained you weren't there, Daisy. Which I don't blame them because you are the best. I'd rather be with you than Angelica too."

I couldn't hide the utter satisfaction that took over the smile on my face. Not only was Andrew realizing he needed me, but so did Angelica.

"You want me to come back to live with you? After you cheated on me in my bed. And now I come back, and you've destroyed my apartment. Not our apartment, Andrew. *Mine*." I pushed my thumb into my chest.

"I haven't destroyed it. Just a few things need to be picked up, that's all. I took care of the grease fire myself. The fire department didn't have to do anything."

"Grease fire? Holy crap." I shook my head as I took in all the craziness. "Andrew, you need to leave. I left before, but now it's your turn."

His mouth fell open, and something fell out of it. I frowned, wondering what it could have been.

"But where will I go? I don't have money or a job."

I shrugged. "That sounds like a you problem, Andrew. This happens when you're so dependent on people to take care of you, and you treat them like shit. At any time, they could stop taking your crap and leave you all alone."

"I didn't treat you like crap, Daisy. I loved you."

"That's love to you? I'd hate to see what you'd do if you disliked someone. I'll give you five minutes to get dressed and grab a bag of clothes. But if you're still here after that, my brother promised to help me remove any pests from my place."

His eyes widened in fear before he quickly nodded and ran back into the bedroom. Andrew was at least smart enough to know that my brother was a man of his word.

Andrew tried to say something as he moved toward the front door once he emerged from the bedroom. But as he was opening his mouth, Lydia said,

"Bye, loser. Don't let the door hit you on the way out. But if it does, it's probably because I kicked it closed on you."

Andrew scurried out like a cockroach.

"Please don't be angry at me, Daisy... but what did you ever see in that man?"

"I don't know. I can only claim temporary blindness. Can someone be legally blind to losers? If so, I had that for two years."

20

CILLIAN

"Where are you?" my dad asked over the phone.

"I'm at home. I wanted a break before the adopt-a-thon tomorrow. Are you at the farm?"

I sat back in my dad's chair. Whenever he wasn't home, which wasn't often, I'd take over his lounger. The thing was old and ugly, but it was the most comfortable seat that ever existed.

"Yes, why wouldn't I be?"

My eyes flickered to the clock that hung on the wall. "Okay. Is Daisy with you?"

It was Friday, and Coach had given us the day off from practice in celebration of beating Seattle. It was a tough game as Seattle had a great team, but we did it.

"Yup, she's here, and so is everyone else."

Did he mean Sam? "Like who?"

"The Devils, for one thing, but Cillian, there's someone here who you will not like."

I rolled my eyes. It was probably Jackson. But if the entire team was there, Jackson wouldn't start anything.

He hadn't been his typical annoying self. In fact, he had been unusually quiet lately. Not wanting to go out with the players after practice, and I swear, he raced to get on his regular clothes after the game to leave as quickly as possible.

"Just tell me. I don't think it will be too big of a surprise, but—"

"It's Shondra." I barely had time to process what my father told me before he continued, "She's here, and she's claiming she's married to you."

I barked out a harsh laugh. "That's ridiculous."

Despite the outrageous lie, there was something tickling the back of my mind—an annoying wiggle of a memory that I was desperate to ignore.

"That's what I thought too. If you two were married, then why did she wait so long to come back and say something?"

"Exactly." I rubbed my forehead.

Why was Shondra at the farm? She wanted something.

Then it hit me. Daisy. Shondra was jealous of Daisy and was there to fuck with her. When she saw the beautiful, sweet woman sharing a table with me at the restaurant a few weeks ago, she couldn't stand it.

That woman always had to have the upper hand. Shondra wanted me to be miserable without her.

"Even if Shondra is lying, you need to get over here. The things she's telling Daisy aren't good."

Shit.

"I'll come straight there."

I ended the call and shoved my phone in my pocket. It took almost no time for me to grab my things and head out the door. Normally it was a twenty-minute drive to the farm, but I got there in half the time. It was dangerous driving the country roads like that, but I knew Shondra was more of a threat.

When I arrived at the farm, I hopped out of my SUV and ran toward the first person I saw, which was Emmanuel. "Hey, what are you doing here?"

His smile widened as he shifted the cardboard box in his arms. "Helping to set up for tomorrow. Me and a few guys wanted to help. Jackson told Daisy, and now we're here."

"Jackson?" I scratched my head.

What was this? Nightmare day? First my ex-girl-friend shows and now Jackson.

Emmanuel tilted his head toward the barn. "Yeah, he's over there with some others. They're cleaning up the horse stalls to turn them into pens for the puppies."

My eyes narrowed. Jackson was here to screw with me. First, he didn't invite me to the strip club—not that I would have gone, but that wasn't the point—and now he was helping with the adopt-a-thon. I bet his idea of help was to ruin it.

I didn't know who to focus on first. Shondra or Jackson?

"Where's Shondra?"

Emmanuel's eyes widened. "She's here?"

I nodded. "My dad called and said she showed up."

"Sorry, dude. I haven't seen her. But I've spent a lot of time cleaning up the farmhouse and haven't been out there."

I took a deep breath. Even the sweet spring air couldn't calm my nerves. "If you see Shondra, tell her I'm looking for her."

"Yes, of course, Cillian. Go out to the barn. Maybe she's there."

"Thanks for helping. That means a lot."

"I'd do anything to help you, Cillian. The entire team would. It excited us when you told us about the adopt-a-thon. Everyone came to me asking if you needed help."

"Why didn't they come to me?"

Emmanuel gave a lopsided smile. "You have a gruff attitude. It's not that they don't like you."

"What?"

"You're rough around the edges, but they still care about you. They understand it was hard when your mom passed, and then you had that terrible break-up with Shondra. So, when you mentioned doing the adopt-a-thon, the team was totally behind you. Just about everyone is here, except for Brian, but I think he's focused on moving to Boston."

I nodded in agreement about Brian before Emmanuel continued, "The past few weeks, it felt like you were finally seeing the light after so much darkness."

"Wow, that was poetic. Didn't know you had that in you."

Emmanuel smiled. "There's a lot about me you don't know."

If the team was rooting for me, then why had I received so many complaints? Especially recently.

He chuckled, and I waved as he moved out to the cars parked in front of the farmhouse.

Nothing made sense. Both Shondra and Jackson were here, and the team was happy to help me. If someone would have told me they'd be here a week ago, I would have called them a liar.

Marching off toward the barn, I waved at Aspen, who was rolling a wheelbarrow filled with old hay and dirt from the barn.

It was true. The more I looked around the farm, the more I saw the guys on the team helping out. I figured Emmanuel had only meant a handful of guys, but so far, I had counted at least ten, and I hadn't stepped foot inside the barn yet.

Who had been complaining about me?

My eyes shifted to the darkened entrance to the barn. The doors were wide open, but the interior remained dark so I couldn't see who was inside. Once I stepped in, I heard a voice as my eyes adjusted to the low lighting.

There was laughter, and I recognized it instantly. Shondra. My nostrils flared as I walked past empty stalls until I found the person I came to see.

"Shondra. Funny running into you again. And at the farm." I folded my arms over my chest.

The only relief I felt was that Shondra was alone. Daisy wasn't with her.

"I read a flyer in town that you were holding an adopt-a-thon at your farm. I thought it was today. But then your girlfriend was nice enough to let me know it starts tomorrow."

"Girlfriend?" I asked, as I didn't want Shondra to know I was with Daisy. If Daisy hadn't said anything, then I might convince Shondra we weren't together.

I knew my ex well. She would make it her mission to destroy me and Daisy. I wasn't about to let that happen. That was probably why she spread that rumor we were married to screw with Daisy.

Shondra tilted her head. "Yes, Daisy. She's so sweet, Cillian. I really am happy for you both."

How would Shondra know about Daisy being my girlfriend? Daisy was adamant about not telling anyone for fear her brother would know.

"You needn't be, as we aren't together. She's just helping me with this." I waved around the barn.

Shondra put her hand over her heart and chuckled. "Oh, what a relief."

I knew she was jealous.

"Happy I'm single, huh, Shondra? Should I still be longing for you? Well, just because Daisy and I aren't together doesn't mean I want you back."

She shook her head. "No, it's something Brian gave me, that's all."

"Brian? The team captain?"

She leaned the rake she was holding against the wall and held out her hand. Her ring finger on her left hand held the biggest diamond and emerald ring I had ever seen.

"That's quite a ring you got there."

"Isn't it gorgeous?" She pulled her hand back and held it as if it was the most precious thing in her world. "He proposed the night I ran into you. It was perfect, overlooking the mountains."

I thought I had seen Brian at the restaurant. "I didn't realize you two were dating."

Her smile widened. "He wanted to keep it secret. It was really sweet, actually. He knew you were hurt because of our breakup and your mother dying, so he felt it best we didn't let anyone know."

I clenched my jaw. "How long have you two been together?"

Her eyes widened. "Oh, gosh, it's such a blur. I think it was..." She let out a nervous giggle and never finished what she said before we were interrupted.

"Hey, Shondra, I found some old gloves for you... Oh, Cillian. You're here?" Daisy walked into the stall.

"Thank you, Daisy. You are such a lifesaver." Shondra took the gloves but kept her eyes bouncing between us. "I told Daisy I'd help. It seemed like such a good cause."

Her smile curled, and not in a good way.

"I just find it strange you two never hooked up," Shondra added.

I swallowed. Where was she going with this?

Daisy laughed nervously. "Why is that so strange? I work for Cillian... nothing more." Daisy raised her voice on the last part.

Glancing around, I noticed Jackson leaning against the opposite stall.

"Then there's nothing to worry about," Shondra said.

"Why would anyone be worried?" I almost didn't want to ask, but it was better to know what she was up to.

She frowned. "Because we're still married, Cillian."

Daisy gasped, and I felt blood rush to my head. Why would she lie like that? Shondra was many things, many terrible things, but she never lied to hurt people.

"No, we are not." I turned to Daisy. "I swear. She's my ex-girlfriend, not my wife."

Jackson strolled toward the stall. "Why is it important that Daisy knows you aren't married? It seems to me it's none of her business."

I ran my hand through my hair. "Yes, of course. But I just wanted to clarify that what Shondra was saying wasn't true."

"But it is true, Cillian." Shondra took a step forward, letting the gloves fall to the ground. "Wow, I didn't think you were that drunk. Remember Vegas? The last night we thought it would be fun to do one of those drive-thru weddings. And it was fun, but I realized my mistake when we sobered up and you turned into a grumpy jerk again. I thought I filed the paperwork for divorce, but I must have forgotten."

"How come I don't remember any of this?"

Shondra folded her arms. "Because you are too self-absorbed to think about anyone but yourself. I thought you never brought it up because I embarrassed you. I mean, we broke up soon after."

"You're married?" Daisy asked, her voice a whisper.

I reached for her, but she stepped back, heartbreak etched in her features.

"I did not know. I swear."

Jackson pulled Daisy behind him and took a step forward. "What the fuck did you do to my sister?"

"I did nothing to her. I love her," I yelled out.

Jackson's eyes grew large, but I wasn't concerned about his reaction. It was the bitter laugh that came from behind him that caused my throat to tighten.

"Love? You don't know what love is, Cillian. You think what we did was love, yet you don't even realize you're married."

I waved my arm back at Shondra. "Neither did she. We both thought we weren't married."

Daisy glared at me with red-rimmed eyes. "But at least she knew you had married once. You couldn't even remember that. Or did you know the whole time, and this is all an act?" She stared up at the ceiling and shook her head. "How do I do it? How do I keep ending up with liars?"

"I'm not a liar. Shondra is the liar."

"How can you say that, Cillian? You know, I would not say this because, unlike you, I don't hold any ill will for you. But calling me a liar, I just can't hold this in."

She turned to Daisy and said, "I knew I recognized your name when we met at the restaurant. I knew it because I remember Cillian made a joke about how you threw up on him. Called you Daisy the Hurler. Told Brian and some others on the team. Brian and I were together by that point, so he told me what Cillian said."

I waved my hands in the air. "That's not true."

But as I watched the scene unfold, Daisy's tears streaming down her face while her brother wrapped his arm around her, the memories came back. Those fucking shitty drunken memories I could never erase despite how much I wanted to.

"Sounds like something you would say, asshat," Jackson said, glaring at me. "You used to come up with nicknames all the time back then. Say shit about the players. That's why I never liked you. And now I really hate your guts after you said that about Daisy." He pushed his finger aggressively into my chest.

Closing my eyes, I drew in a breath. It felt like my last because, in the next moment, I'd drown. I couldn't lie to Daisy. She didn't deserve it.

"I said that about you, Daisy. It's not an excuse, but I was drunk and hurt. I thought you didn't like me and…" I glanced at her brother, not caring what he did to me after I admitted what came from my heart, "I had the biggest crush on you since I first met you."

"What the fuck?" Jackson ground out.

I held up my hands. "Let me finish before you beat the crap out of me. Back when I was drinking, I was so conceited, thought I was the best at everything—hockey, women, you name it."

I frowned and shook my head. I was an asshole and deserved everything that came my way.

"When you puked on me, I was stunned. I couldn't believe someone would do that and then run away from me. Honestly, I was probably the one who let it out that we kissed. But I don't remember because of the drinking. I have a feeling Shondra is telling the truth."

Daisy stepped back, her hand covering her mouth.

"I'm sorry, but I don't remember."

She ran off, leaving me in the stall with two people who wanted to kill me. The way I felt, it would be a blessing if they went through with it.

21

DAISY

"This is awkward," Angelica said as she stared at Cillian, showing someone a puppy.

I let out a sigh and felt like I was living a nightmare.

Nope, just the adopt-a-thon I helped plan. Then the guy I thought was my boyfriend but turned out to be married was about twenty yards away at the same event.

What nightmare wouldn't be complete without my ex-boss showing up too?

"How did you find out that Cillian and I broke up?" I turned to look at her perfect cheekbones and felt my stomach start to reject the coffee I had earlier.

"Cillian? Who's Cillian?"

I pointed to the man she had been gazing at.

"Not that guy, the one behind him. Andrew."

I threw my hands up in the air and yelled out, "Fuck."

A few heads turned my way; one woman even pursed her lips and covered her little girl's ears.

I winced. "Sorry." The woman sneered at me and tugged the little girl away from the dog she had been petting.

"Fuck is right. I hate when I run into a guy I slept with. They are always begging me to come back. It's pathetic."

I smirked at the knowledge that Andrew had already done that with me. Even if he asked Angelica back today, I knew he had begged me first.

Pinching my brow, I groaned. Was I thrilled at the petty thought of being Andrew's first pick? Yesterday had been so bad that, yes, I was taking joy out of it. It was sad, but it was my pathetic win.

"I know. It was so sad when Andrew asked me back last week. So sad."

Angelica coughed and took a step back. "Wh-what? He asked you back?"

I nodded, not even bothering to look at her. "Oh, yes. He appeared so pathetic in my robe. Like he missed me so much that he had to wear my clothes."

"But you're so, uh..."

I turned toward Angelica. Her face was pale, as if she had seen a ghost. Folding my arms, I asked, "I'm so what?"

Before she could answer, Cillian's father came over. "Daisy. This is going great. We've adopted five dogs already, and it's not even lunchtime." He had a big grin on his face, but I couldn't help but notice the pity twinkling in his eyes.

Cillian must have told him about how we ended things. As much as it hurt to discover Cillian had been married the whole time, it broke my heart when he denied being involved with me to Shondra.

It shouldn't have hurt, but it did. I was the one who told him to deny our relationship to everyone, but to hear it out loud... it felt so real.

"Wonderful. We have to keep up the good work."

Mr. Walsh nodded but kept glancing over at Angelica. "Pardon me for asking, but why are you here?" He glared at my former boss.

"I used to be a part of the adopt-a-thon in previous years, so—"

Putting my hand on her shoulder, I stopped Angelica. "Oh, don't be so modest. No, she's here to beg me back. It seems when she fired me, people stopped bring their pets to her clinic. Now she's lucky to get a sick bird."

Angelica cleared her throat, apparently unhappy with my new-found zero-fucks-given attitude. She didn't want me informing Cillian's dad the real reason she showed up at his farm.

Tough titties, Angelica. Don't go sleeping with my man behind my back.

"I wouldn't say 'beg,' but I do—"

"But you were tearing up when you were asking me back. Saying how lost you were without me. And the clinic will close within the next month if I don't come back. Then there was the moment you were on your knees—"

185

"Hey, I fell. I just shouldn't have worn heels to a farm. It wasn't like I was begging. And if this is your attitude, then maybe I don't need you back after all."

It was fun messing with Angelica. She deserved all the humiliation I had thrust upon her. But she had come at a perfect time since I wouldn't be working for Cillian anymore.

I had already worked for someone who had no problem lying and using me. I couldn't do that again.

Going back to work for Angelica wasn't a better option, but since I didn't care about Andrew anymore, it wouldn't break my heart every time I stepped foot into the clinic.

"She wouldn't go back to you if you paid her double." Mr. Walsh folded his arms over his rounded belly.

Angelica's eyes flashed with determination. I knew that look—she got it whenever a client questioned her methods. "Actually, I was going to pay her double—and offer her a full-time veterinarian position."

My brow rose. "Really? Because I would like—"

"That's nothing." Mr. Walsh stepped forward. "She doesn't need to be a vet at some tiny clinic. She's the vet to all the local farm animals and the Blue Ridge Mountain Devils mascot, Willy the goat."

I was?

Angelica took a step forward, folding her arms over her gigantic boobs. Their elbows butted up against each other, much like two rams in a fight.

"You didn't let me finish. I'm prepared to offer her—"

I slowly backed away, and neither of them noticed. Both were making up deals they offered me, only to out-do each other.

"Why is she here?" Lydia's voice came from behind.

I turned and flung my arms around my best friend. "I'm so sorry to hear about your grandmother. You really didn't have to come here today. I would have understood."

Her grandma passed away last week, the day after she help me kick Andrew out of my apartment. That was why she hadn't been around to help with the adopt-a-thon.

She let out a breath, and I felt her deflate in my arms. I held her until she was ready to let go.

"A chance to be around lots of adorable animals and hot hockey players...? I don't know of a better distraction than that."

I had to agree this was a wonderful distraction. The only problem was that the hot hockey player I kept focusing on was the one who broke my heart.

"I heard about Cillian. Damn, I'm so sorry. That was shitty."

"I must have some pheromone that attracts assholes. That's the only logical explanation I have for these guys."

She threw her arm around me and walked me toward the house, where all the cats and kittens were.

When we got inside, I saw one of the tall hockey players with Fierce in his arms. He seemed taken with the cat, and I hoped they made a match. I knew Sophia wasn't going to be happy with Fierce gone, no matter how much she pretended she wasn't in love with the cat.

She took me upstairs, and we walked into a bed-room.

"I'm not sure we should be in here," I said. Now that Cillian and I weren't together, it felt strange walking around his childhood home.

"It's fine. I asked Mr. Walsh if he had any towels, and he told me there were some in this closet. When I opened the closet door, I found some towels, but I also found this..." She pointed to a photograph pinned to a wall inside the closet.

There were a few pictures pinned up. But the one Lydia pointed at was of me, Jackson, Aspen, and right behind us was Cillian. He had a beer can in his hand that he held up like a trophy and was making a funny face.

He seemed happy—drunk, but happy. But it wasn't who was in the photograph that caught my attention, it was what had been written on it.

There was a heart that circled me, and off to the side, someone had written *I wish she knew the real me*.

Maybe that was the problem... He only ever showed me his secrets and lies.

"I wish I knew the real Cillian, but I don't." I turned and reached in to grab a towel that Lydia must have missed. Animals overran the place. We'd need all the towels we could get.

"I think you do, Daisy."

Taking a step back, I turned to face her. "No, I don't. He lied about everything. He was married, Lydia. That's fucked-up."

"I agree with you. It's messed up. But he had a lot of problems back then. Just because someone has demons they're fighting doesn't mean you don't help them."

I threw up my arms. "That's for him and Shondra to figure out."

"How did they break up?"

I explained she didn't want to be around him while he grieved.

"Hmm, well... that's terrible."

I nodded. "Totally agree. It's not that I think she's a saint, but you don't leave someone when they're down."

"Isn't that what I just said?"

I tilted my head. "No, you said try to help someone you love when they're hurting."

"Do you think it hurt Cillian? You told me he didn't remember being married to Shondra. He's probably freaking out right now. I know I would be."

"Yeah, I guess." I nibbled my bottom lip. "But he called me a terrible name. I bet the job here was guilt because of that. He was trying to do all those nice things because he knew what an asshole he was."

Lydia sighed. "You're probably right. Gosh, what a terrible thing to do. To regret the things he did back when he struggled with addiction and try to make amends. Try to help the person he hurt." Her lips thinned, and I didn't appreciate her sarcasm.

"He's married, Lydia. Even if I can forgive what he did, he's a married man. He may not remember, but the law doesn't forget. Yes, Shondra's a horrible person, but I'm not about to *Angelica* her."

Lydia snorted. "Please tell me we are now referring to anyone who takes part in a cheating relationship as an *Angelica*."

I nodded. "Angelica for a woman, and Andrew for a guy."

She gave me a chef's kiss. "Perfection."

It felt good to talk about what happened with my best friend. What she said made sense, but it didn't change the fact that Cillian was a married man.

22

CILLIAN

I stared at the glass of amber liquid that sat on the dark wooden bar in front of me. A ripple sliced over the drink as someone sat on the stool next to me.

"How many have you had?" he asked.

I made a circle with my fingers. "Zero. I'm taking my time with this one."

"Okay, then how many sips have you had?" he asked the more important question.

Holding up my hand again, I said, "Zero. Really taking my time."

"Hmm. So, you're a coward."

My nose flared as I tilted my head toward Jackson.

"Fuck you." I pointed to my eye that was almost completely swollen shut. "You had your chance with me yesterday at the farm. I don't know why you were so angry. You got what you wanted. Daisy hates me and wants nothing to do with me. Why don't you just leave me to stare at this glass of whiskey?"

"Nah, I don't think I will." He slapped me hard on my back, causing me to wince. "I was just telling Aspen how I needed to come to Castle Moat to stare at some drinks. Just stare."

I groaned. Why was he such an annoying jerk?

Rubbing my face, careful to avoid my black eye, I turned my attention back to the glass.

"Maybe I'll order one so I have my own glass to stare at."

I rolled my good eye. "Has anyone told you that you act like a child?"

"Has anyone told you that you're a grumpy dick?"

I shifted my gaze toward him. He had a shit-eating grin on his face, while I had the insane urge to punch him. Make his lip as swollen as my eye.

"All the fucking time. Now go home."

"I can't." He shrugged. "Why don't *you* go home?"

So damn childish.

"Because I want to be here. I want to be surrounded by all the things that ever brought happiness to my life. I tried the sober road, and it sucked!"

The bartender looked over, as did the other people sitting at the bar.

"It sucked. For me."

"You're an alcoholic, Jackson?"

He shook his head. "No, I'm not talking about me. I'm saying you being sober sucked for me. You were the biggest asshole when you drank. The guys hated hanging out with you. Brian the most."

"Brian?" I knew he wasn't my biggest fan, but I didn't think he hated me.

"Yeah, we'd all talk shit about you all the time. And when you kissed my sister, which, it was actually Brian who told me, by the way…"

Huh. I felt better knowing that.

"Anyway, it was easier to hate you when you were the jerk everyone disliked. But then you had to sober up. Your annoyingness turned to grumpiness, and, to the guys, you became someone to look up to."

"That can't be true." I smirked because he thought I was dumb enough to fall for his crap.

"Seriously. They saw how you had to deal with your mom's death, and then you sobered up. You became the model hockey player—tough but wise. God, I hated you for that."

I stared at Jackson. His jaw tightened, and I knew he was telling the truth. Then a thought formed in my head. Something that made total sense, and I itched to punch Jackson again.

"Then I guess you were the one who was complaining about me to Coach. You know, I almost got kicked off the team because of you."

He turned toward me and held up his hand. "Whoa. I never complained about anyone to Coach. That's a dick move. As much as you annoyed me, you're still my teammate, and I'll always have your back."

"Then who was it?" I muttered, rubbing the back of my neck.

"I have a feeling I might know..." Jackson said, waving the bartender away when he walked up to him.

I stared at him, but he didn't say a thing.

"I'm not looking at you for my health. Who do you think complained about me?"

"Brian."

"Really? He was never mean to me. Some players said some shitty things to me when we lost a game or they were hungover at practice, but he never did."

Jackson leaned closer. "Brian kept starting rumors about you, then he secretly started dating Shondra behind your back."

I gripped the brass railing of the bar and shifted to face Jackson. "What? You mean, while I was still with Shondra?"

He nodded. "It was right after the party when Daisy threw up on you when I discovered it. We ran into Shondra at the coffee shop. I went to order our coffee while he talked to her. I thought he was just being polite. Then he told me you kissed Daisy, and I was furious. He suggested we mess with you, and I was really considering it. Brian said he never liked how you treated the guys, so he had already fucked with you. He told me he had secretly been dating her for almost six months. By that time, you two had only been broken up two or three months."

"What a fucking asshole."

"I told him he shouldn't have done that, and he should admit it to you. It may have angered you, but honesty was better than secrets. But I didn't press him too hard. I was angry you tried to kiss Daisy, so I did nothing about it. I'm sorry."

I placed my hand on his shoulder. "It's okay. I forgive you. Things were messed up back then."

"But what he did never sat well with me. I stopped believing the rumors he told about you. But he didn't realize that; he thought I still liked him."

"Thanks for telling me. You didn't need to come down here to let me know. You could have told me at practice tomorrow. Besides, Brian is leaving, and I couldn't be happier."

"I dropped out of the running for team captain."

My mouth fell open. Jackson had just as good a chance as I did to be team captain. Some would say he had a better chance. Why would he drop out?

"Don't do that because of me."

He tilted his eyes toward me. "Don't flatter yourself, Grumpy Old Man."

Ah, the nickname the players had made for me... After the crappy things I had done to them, I deserved that name.

"I'm not doing it for you, Cillian. There is a reason I don't want to be team captain. Something I will announce at a later date, but just know it would take my focus away from my duties as team captain. I'd never be able to arrange an event like the adopt-a-thon with what I'm planning."

More secrets.

"Haven't you learned from my debacle that secrets always end badly?"

"Nope. You know me, Cillian." He tapped his head with his fist. "It takes a lot for me to learn something."

"Then I guess I'll be team captain. Unless you know someone else who might run?"

He shook his head. "There's something else I need to tell you, Cillian. Something that's a little hard to say."

"You said that same thing to me yesterday, right before you punched me."

"I will not hit you, I mean it. When I started suspecting you and Daisy were seeing each other, I didn't like it. But I could understand why my sister wanted to be with you. Out of everyone on the team, you're the best. And you're not a player with women. I knew you'd do right by Daisy."

"How did you know we were together?"

"My sister is wonderful at many things, but lying isn't one of them. It was great when we were growing up. I'd win at all the card and board games. But when she started dating..." The muscle in his jaw flexed. "I'll just say it was obvious when she was going to sneak out with a guy."

I already knew they had lost their dad when Daisy was just a teenager, and Jackson had to take over as the parent for her. It couldn't have been easy being a big brother and father to a teenage girl.

"You're a good brother," I said and gave him a nod.

He took a breath, as if he needed a moment to process my words. Jackson placed his hand on my shoulder. "You're a good son. Take it from someone who's a father."

I clenched my jaw and turned my gaze to the alcohol bottles lining the shelf. I didn't know if I was a good son, but I loved my parents. And I missed the hell out of my mom.

"Not always, but I'm trying to do better." My voice wobbled, so I cleared my throat.

"I can't believe I'm about to say this, but I think you need to get back together with my sister."

I blinked, unsure of what he just told me. "I must be hearing things, Jackson. It sounded like you *want* me to get back with Daisy."

He nodded. "Yes, please don't make me repeat it."

"I don't think that's a good idea." I reached for the glass out of habit before Jackson snatched it out of my hand.

"Don't do this." He held up the drink to the bartender. "He's done."

The bartender nodded and took the whiskey away.

"Your job's done. You took away the drink and told me I am basically team captain. Jackson, you are the hero. You can go home."

"Not until I tell you the truth about your marriage."

My head shot back in surprise. How would Jackson know anything about the Vegas wedding?

Memories surfaced after Shondra explained our nuptials. I remembered us being outside a chapel in Las Vegas and thinking it was the funniest idea.

My stomach churned with the memory of me getting on one knee to propose to Shondra with a mint wrapper I had in my pocket. I had twisted it to form a ring.

I wanted Shondra to be a liar, but she wasn't. I had been married this whole time.

"I already know. I'm married. That's why I'm sitting here trying to get drunk. To forget about the stupid mistake I made."

Jackson slapped my shoulder again. "You're not married, Cillian. You're *divorced*."

23

DAISY

"While I'm happy to see you again, I really hoped you'd never come back," Diana said with a frown.

"Wow, glad to see you too."

I walked into the veterinarian clinic on my first official day back. It was Monday, and the adopt-a-thon was a success. We adopted out every single pet that had been up for adoption, which was a first in the history of the adopt-a-thon.

My guess was some players were big animal lovers and couldn't bear the idea of the animals going back to the rescue. Cillian's dad told me Aspen ended up with three dogs and two cats.

There was an anonymous donor who doubled whatever proceeds the rescue made from the event. I would have been jumping for joy if I hadn't kept running into Cillian.

"I didn't mean it like that. I meant Angelica had it coming. She deserved to fail. But then it would mean I'd lose my job, so as much as I wanted to never see you back here, I'm glad you're here."

I didn't know whether to be happy or hurt by that statement.

"I'm back, and I got a huge pay raise. I'll be head veterinarian. Plus, she's promised to get me coffee from Hard Grind every morning."

I gave a smug smile at the pretty sweet deal I got from Mr. Walsh's haggling. Once he told me that was what he was doing, I was grateful. I might have been more confident now, but job negotiation wasn't my strong suit.

Diana frowned.

"What's wrong? I thought you'd like it. She has to get me coffee every day. Maybe I can make her get some for you too."

"It's not that." She nibbled on her purple lip. "It's that she called out... for the week."

"What? She won't be here? Did she leave money or a gift card for the coffee?" It wasn't a big deal, but I loved the idea of getting free coffee.

"No. She didn't tell me anything. Just that there was a veterinarian starting, and the new vet would be in charge while she was away. Angelica didn't even say it was you coming in."

My shoulders sagged. God, I was such an idiot. I thought she had wised up, but no. I was doing the same thing I did before, but at least now for more money.

I guess the bigger paycheck was a good thing.

Diana held up her finger. "Wait. She left this envelope."

She pulled out a white envelope from a drawer in her desk with the word "veterinarian" written on it. Ugh. She couldn't even be bothered to write my name.

I plucked it out of Diana's hand and ripped it open.

Daisy,

I thought about our arrangement and need to speak to my lawyer about it. While I am glad to have you back, there are costs of having another employee. I don't think I can agree to my original offer. How about an extra dollar? I think that seems fair.

Your boss,

Angelica.

"A dollar? I am only getting an extra dollar?" I stared at the paper, hoping I read it wrong.

Nope. She only wrote a dollar.

"An extra dollar an hour isn't bad. I'd like to make an extra dollar an hour," Diana said.

"Yes, an extra dollar an hour would be nice." I crumpled up the paper and threw it near the wastebin, and it bounced off the edge of the can and slid into the corner. There it would stay until, hopefully, a dog peed on it.

"But since I am a salaried employee, she only means I am making an extra dollar a year, not an hour."

Diana's eyes widened, but before she could say anything, the door to the clinic flew open, and Mr. Walsh came in out of breath.

I raced over to him as he clutched at his chest. "Are you alright? Should I call an ambulance?"

He shook his head but couldn't speak. I led him over to one of the waiting room chairs. He sat down and mouthed the word "water."

I glanced over at Diana, who was already rushing over with a water bottle.

After a few sips, Mr. Walsh spoke, "I am really out of shape."

"Do you want me to call your doctor? Is your arm numb, or does it have shooting pains?" I might have been a veterinarian, but I knew enough about human medicine to help until the medics arrived.

"I'm not having a heart attack." He looked at me as if I just threw the bottle of water in his face.

"That's good."

"I ran here from your apartment and realized I need to exercise again."

"Why were you at my apartment?"

He gave me an exasperated look. "To take you to work? Sam's waiting."

"But I work here now. Remember?" I glanced over at Diana with worry. Was he having a stroke? "You were the one who negotiated my salary."

I wasn't about to tell him it was all for nothing since Angelica was reneging on the deal.

"If that's what you want?" He stood, and I grabbed his arm to help. He waved me away but stumbled before righting himself.

"I guess we'll just have to find someone else to help with all those homeless animals that are coming over from Big Mountain Animal Rescue."

My god, he was having a stroke. That had already happened.

"Mr. Walsh... those animals came over two days ago, on Saturday, for the adopt-a-thon. It's over."

He shoved his hand on his hip. "I know all those animals were adopted. But the new ones they got yesterday and today will be showing up at the farm. The Big Mountain Animal Rescue building is closing up shop. Those animals have to go somewhere."

I gasped, covering my mouth with my hand. The rescue was closing? No...

"But why? Why are they closing?"

I must have asked the wrong question because Mr. Walsh was more annoyed with me than when I tried to help him out of the chair.

"You ask too many questions. Just come to the farm and find out for yourself. And since we are asking questions, why are you working here?"

I was completely confused. Nothing this man said made sense.

"Because Angelica asked me back."

"But you had a great job that paid better than this."

I couldn't believe Cillian hadn't told his father about what happened on Saturday with Shondra.

Cillian had faults, but I never pegged him as a coward.

"I thought it best to come back here."

His lips thinned. "No, you didn't. You just didn't want to see my son because he did some stupid things many years ago."

I guess he had told his father.

"You're right." I let out a breath. "I'm just tired of working for liars."

"Then I ask you again, why are working here?"

I ran my hand over my face. "Because there's nothing else. I want to work with animals. I don't want to be a barista or a receptionist or an accountant, which are all perfectly fine jobs for other people. Here, I get to work with animals. I get to care for them when they can't care for themselves."

He smiled. "Now was that so hard to admit?"

"No..." I said, very much confused by his line of questioning.

He waved me out the door. I told Diana I'd be back in a little while, and if it was an emergency, to tell the client to head to the farm.

It was a quick five-minute walk to my apartment building where Sam's car waited. The men gave each other knowing looks. I tried to find out what was going on, but Mr. Walsh muttered about too many questions.

When we made it to the farm, I saw there were several cars parked out front. I got out and heard the bleat of a goat.

As we moved closer, I caught a whiff of something delicious. That was unusual for a farm, as it normally smelled of manure, animals, and hay.

"Am I imagining it, or is someone cooking?" I asked Mr. Walsh.

"Someone is cooking. It's getting close to lunchtime, so I made sure there would be food."

It wasn't even ten in the morning. My eyes slid to Cillian's father. No matter my feelings about Cillian, I was going to have to reach out to him and let him know I believed his father should see a doctor.

"Yes, lunchtime. Mmm." I rubbed my belly.

Maybe he wanted to thank me for helping his son with the adopt-a-thon. I smiled. It was sweet of him to go to these lengths to thank me.

"Look, Mr. Walsh, if you just want to thank—" My words died on my lips when Cillian stepped out of the house with my brother behind him.

"What is going on?" I mumbled to myself.

Why was my brother grinning and throwing his arm around Cillian?

"Daisy. Great, you're here," Jackson called out and moved down the three steps from the farmhouse to the ground.

Cillian stayed at the front door. He knew enough to keep his distance.

"Why, Jackson? Can someone please tell me why I am here?"

Jackson glanced back at Cillian, who turned and went back inside. *Run away, coward. Run away.*

"Welcome to your new job." Jackson waved his hands around the farm.

My brows shot up. "Has everyone gone mad? I don't work for Cillian anymore. I work at the veterinarian clinic in Castle Ridge."

"Walk with me, Sis." Jackson put his hand on my shoulder and pushed me forward. I stumbled but didn't fall.

"I have my own legs and don't need to be forced into walking."

"Didn't you always dream of having an animal sanctuary on a farm?"

"Yeah, but what does that... Wait a minute. Don't tell me Cillian is giving me this farm out of pity?" I cupped my hands around my mouth and yelled toward the farmhouse door, "Because I don't accept pity gifts."

Mr. Walsh strolled by, heading toward the farmhouse door. "It's my farm, and I'm not selling it to anyone."

Poor Sam was walking beside him and shoved his hands into his jeans pockets, not knowing where to look. The boy was clearly uncomfortable.

"I'm not working for Cillian, if that's why I'm here. And if Cillian wants to hire me, then why isn't he out here talking to me?"

My brother said something, but I cut him off. I was fed up with the excuses men gave me for being selfish pricks.

"He's not here because he's a coward. He screwed up marrying someone and didn't even try to find out what happened while he was in Vegas. I may not have ever been blackout drunk before, because I don't think I physically can, but I've been with people who have. And they always ask what happened the next day. They *want* to know. Why didn't he want to know, Jackson? Hmm? Answer me that."

Again, Jackson talked, but I marched off toward the farmhouse door. I knew he was going to feed me another excuse that made no sense. It was time to find the truth from the man himself.

I slammed my feet on the white wooden steps that led to the door. Grabbing the red door, I pushed, and when I stepped inside, my mouth almost hit the floor.

Everyone I knew and most of the Devils were in the house. Even Sophia stood in the kitchen, cooking something. That was where the wonderful smells were coming from.

I craned my neck but didn't see Cillian. There was food and some soft music playing in the background. This was obviously a celebration.

An arm slipped into mine, and I jerked back in surprise. I let out a sigh of relief when I realized it was Lydia. "Girl, you scared me."

"Sorry. But I wanted to welcome you to your Dream Come True Party."

"Why is there a party for me at Mr. Walsh's farmhouse?" I held up my finger. "No excuses. Everyone I ask has given me the runaround. I need the truth."

She gave me a soft smile. "The Big Mountain Animal Rescue has closed its doors."

"I know, I heard. Isn't it awful? And after they had such an amazing adoption rate with the adopt-a-thon."

She shook her head. "No, they just closed their location. They will move here. And since you did such a wonderful job with the adopt-a-thon, they want to hire you as their animal medical director. I don't know the specifics, but you'd work here with the animals. Oh, and Mr. Walsh is converting the barn into a veterinarian clinic. That way any procedures the animals need can be done right here."

I glanced around, wondering if this was some sort of joke, as it seemed a little too perfect to be real.

"If they want me to have the job, why haven't they offered it themselves? I would think they'd want to interview me."

Lydia stepped back and tilted her head. "Are you serious? You just found out about your dream job coming true, and you don't believe it? You've been volunteering there for years. They know you. They have everything they need to know about you. I'm sure if you ask, they can interview you."

I folded my arms, still uneasy about all this. Why did Lydia know and not me?

"I didn't get a call from them..."

She lifted something from her back pocket and held it in front of me. "You mean this phone? The one you left here after the adopt-a-thon? Mr. Walsh gave it to me because, when he showed up at your apartment yesterday, you weren't there. I tried to find you too, but no Daisy."

I chewed on my lower lip. "I hid out at the coffee shop all day. It's where I go to drink my troubles away."

She frowned. "With coffee?"

"Yes. I don't recommend it. But that still doesn't answer the question, why you know about the job and I don't."

"They called while I had the phone. I hoped it was you trying to locate your phone, but it was them. They explained they were informed that the farm location was up for rent, and they took it. They created a position that was part-veterinarian, part-coordinator, and they instantly thought of you for that position."

"But I haven't said yes to the job yet, and to be perfectly honest, if I have to work here, I don't know if I will. It's like moving from working under the roof of one person who hurt me to another. I just can't do that. Even for a dream job."

I let out a sigh and turned to make my way to door. That was when I ran into my brother.

"Daisy, you're making a mistake."

"No, Jackson. For the first time in my life, I'm standing up for my heart. It's been bruised and battered too much, and it needs to heal. Even if that means working for those spoiled billionaires at The Blue Spot."

Because I wasn't even going back to the veterinarian clinic. Fuck Angelica and her dollar raise.

I pushed past Jackson. As I opened the door, I heard him say, "Cillian isn't married. He's divorced."

24

DAISY

I turned back and closed the door. Moving back into the entranceway of the farmhouse, I asked, "What do you mean, he's divorced?"

"Brian and Shondra set out to screw with Cillian. I think Shondra did it because she's a bitch. I know something about exes being bitches, so I knew it the moment I met her." Jackson chuckled.

"What about Brian? Isn't that her fiancé and your team captain?"

"Ex-captain. I informed Coach yesterday exactly what Brian had pulled, and he was fired instantly. Brian said he didn't care; that it was worth messing with Cillian. Apparently, Cillian made up a nickname for Brian back when he was drinking, and he found out about it. After that, Brian was hellbent on ruining Cillian."

My eyes widened. "That's terrible, but it doesn't explain the divorce."

"Yup, Cillian got married in Vegas. The reason he didn't remember isn't because he was drunk; it's because Shondra spiked his drink."

I took a step back. "Wait. I'm confused. How would anyone know that except for Shondra? You saw Cillian Saturday when she told him... He has no memory of the wedding. He would have had to get his blood tested to know. Two years is way too late to have your blood tested for being roofied or whatever she used on him."

"Benzos. At least, that's what she told me." My brother's lips curled into an evil grin. "The reason I know is because I got suspicious after what she said in the barn on Saturday. Having been married to Katie, I swear I can sniff out the gold-diggers."

I sighed, but Jackson continued, "I played it up that I was on her side. She invited me over to dinner with herself and Brian. That's when they let it all slip because they thought I hated Cillian. They told me how Shondra tricked him into marriage by spiking his drink. Then, when his mother died and he became boring—her words, not mine—she divorced him. She got him to sign the document by tricking him into thinking it was about a car loan. So they really did get divorced. But when she saw you in the restaurant and Brian found out, they decided to screw with Cillian one last time."

"She lied. My god, she said those things just to hurt Cillian." Sucking in a breath, I couldn't believe what I had done. "And I ran away. He wasn't the asshole... I was."

My brother pulled me in for a hug. "It's like you've finally accepted what I've been telling you all your life."

I pulled away and gave him a playful shove as he chuckled.

"Where is he?"

He pointed up. I ran to the stairs and took them double-time. Walking into the room I assumed was once his—the one with those pictures in the closet—I found Cillian. He held a photograph in his hands but looked up when I stepped inside the room.

"I'm sorry," I said, wrapping my arms around myself. "I know that isn't enough, but I really am so sorry. I should have believed you. It's just that—"

He took a few steps toward me, and I caught a whiff of his spicy cologne. My fingers itched to reach out to him. It had only been two days, but I missed him so much.

"Don't apologize. You had every right to feel hurt. You thought I lied to you. How were you to know I was drugged or that Shondra was lying? Or that Brian was super crazy?"

"I know, right? What the hell was up with him? That's psycho behavior."

He nodded. "The coach informed Boston, and now he will not be on that team either. No hockey team wants him. And Jackson told me if I wanted to go to the police with what Shondra did, he'd back me up." Cillian's hand lifted, and he pushed a stray hair behind my ear. A shiver ran down my neck at his touch.

"Are you going to press charges?"

He took another step forward until I felt the heat of his body against mine. I leaned into him, resting my head on his chest. His hand came up, running his fingers through my hair.

All the stress from the past few days drifted away as I melted into his arms.

"You better believe I'm pressing charges. What she did was insane."

I chuckled and slid my arms around Cillian. He let out a soft groan, and the rumble ran down to my core.

"Daisy, I need you to know something." He stiffened. "I swear I had nothing to do with the job offer."

I nodded, my forehead rubbing against his chest. "I know. Lydia explained everything."

"I did, however, help my dad reach out to the Big Mountain Animal Rescue to let them know his property was available to rent at a much cheaper price than what they were paying."

My arms tightened around his waist. "Thank you," I whispered.

The Walshes were good men. Cillian helped with the adopt-a-thon by bringing the Devils in on it, and his father was renting his farm to the animal rescue. They seemed to put their money where their heart lay.

"Are you going to take the job?"

As I processed all that had happened, I let out a breath. "I would be stupid not to. It's a dream come true."

Cillian pulled back, holding me at arm's length. "That's the last thing you are… stupid. You're the smartest, sweetest woman I know. Your gift is your heart. The care you put into what you do, for animals and for the people around you. But I understand if you don't take the job, and I would never call you stupid for that decision."

"Are you going to be here? I mean, when the Big Mountain Animal Rescue moves in."

"I don't live here, so no. And if you don't want me to stop by ever, I won't."

"It's your father's home and the place where you grew up. I could never ask that of you."

The corner of his mouth curved. "There you go again, being kind. Thinking only of another person's comfort and not your own."

I slid my finger down his chest. "I am being selfish. Working here would be a lot more enjoyable if you came to visit. Maybe we could take a stroll and go visit that fence we inspected several weeks ago."

Cillian's eyes rounded with hope as he cupped my face. "You don't hate me anymore?"

"You may be grumpy at times, but I could never hate you. In fact… I love you."

His eyes softened, and he leaned his head toward mine. For a moment, I thought he was going to kiss me, but he stopped right before his lips reached mine.

"Let's make a promise. No matter what happens, we talk about it. Even if it's a hard topic to discuss, we don't run off or keep it buried inside."

"That sounds like a wise idea. There's something I would like to discuss right now."

"Really? What?"

"Why are your lips not on mine? It has been days since they had a workout. I think they need their exercise."

Cillian chuckled, but before I could continue my point, he captured my mouth with his. Tingles ran through my body, and I dug my fingers into his sides.

His mouth broke free only to travel down my neck. My eyes burned with happy tears, accompanied by a bubble of laughter.

"You know what else I love? Your mouth on my body. Let's discuss."

He groaned and lifted his head. "I was serious, and now you're making fun of me."

"I love the idea, but it's the timing I'm making fun of."

His lips thinned. "I'll give you that. Maybe I should have mentioned it right as I was about to give you an orgasm with my tongue."

Right as I was about to tell him to test out his idea on me, someone cleared their throat behind us.

"Now that you two have made up, can we eat?" Mr. Walsh stood there with his arms folded. "That food smells spectacular, and my stomach is waging a war with me over it."

"Why can't you eat it? Did Sophia say something?" My gaze bounced between Mr. Walsh and his son.

"No. My stubborn son told everyone they couldn't eat until you joined the party."

"Don't hold off on my account. Sophia is an amazing cook. Go, enjoy. It's your home."

Mr. Walsh glared and pointed at his son. "Exactly. Listen to her. She knows what she's talking about." Then he turned and left.

"I guess we should join the party," Cillian said as he dotted kisses on the back of my neck.

I sighed, leaning back into him. "I guess we should."

His hands drifted from my belly up to cup my breast. Arching into his touch, I wondered if we might get in a quickie before going downstairs.

Cillian must have had the same thought as his other hand slipped under the waistband of my pants. I reached my arm back, letting my fingers slip into his silky hair.

But all of it ended when his father shouted, "Get down here. Someone ordered pizza, and the chef isn't thrilled."

My shoulders slumped as Cillian stepped away. "We better get started before there's a pizza fight," I said, grabbing Cillian's hand.

"They better not do anything to that pizza. Maybe I can hide it, and we can have it later, after everyone leaves."

I hugged his arm right as we stepped out of the room. "And I can feed you slices... naked."

"You just described my fantasy."

Turning to face him, I stood on my tiptoes and kissed the tip of his nose. "There will be lots of time for us to explore all our fantasies. But now, it's time to enjoy the party, together."

25

CILLIAN

Cillian
    Jackson's lips curled into a wicked grin.

I shook my head. "Don't." My gaze bounced between Jackson, Aspen, Teddy, and who I thought was a friend but was turning out to be a traitor, Emmanuel.

"Oh, yes." Aspen nodded, but overdid it, making him look like a bobblehead.

They surrounded me, and there was nothing I could do to escape.

"Does Coach know about this?" I asked, hoping they would stop.

"He's the one who told us about it. Oh, this is going to be fun," Emmanuel said.

My heart pounded in my chest. The space between them gave me ideas of how to escape, but they shrank the closer they came, and my time to leave grew shorter.

"This seems childish."

"You already told me I acted like a child, and I didn't disagree with you," Jackson said as he stood right in front of me. Teddy had slipped behind me while Aspen and Emmanuel stood on either side.

I swallowed. It was too late.

"Get him," Jackson said, and I instantly felt their hands on my body.

Fingers poked and scratched, and I tried to push them away, but they were quick.

"Stop," I called out as a smile grew on my face—a grin that I hated. Then a chuckle bubbled up and out of my throat. I was coughing and laughing and couldn't stop.

"His neck. Damn, he's super ticklish there." I didn't know who said it because I was overcome with sensation.

I didn't mind the odd tickle, but to be bombarded like that... it was unbearable.

"Okay, guys, knock it off. He's had enough."

The only person on my side got them to stop.

Daisy.

Their hands slipped away, and I melted to the damp floor, heaving for air.

"We're just hazing him. It's a ritual, Daisy. Once someone makes team captain, we bombarded them with tickles," Jackson said.

I lifted my head and watched the woman I loved stare the four large hockey players down. After a few seconds, they hung their heads and made excuses about having to leave.

A hand appeared in front of my face. I took it and stood, but I didn't let go. Pulling Daisy into my arms, I said, "Thanks. Normally, I'd be able to defend myself, but as you know, tickling is my weakness."

A sexy grin appeared on her face. "I know."

"Why are you at the rink? I was just about to leave so I could stop by the farm to see how the opening day with the Big Mountain Animal Rescue went." I wrapped my arm around her shoulder as we made our way toward the front door of the ice rink.

The Devils had their last practice of the season today, and the coach announced I was the new team captain. We didn't make it to the Cup finals, but with me as captain, I told them I'd work hard to make sure we made it next season. It surprised me when all the guys cheered. It was going to take me a while until I trusted that they didn't hate me.

"It was great. We got a bunch of adorable puppies and kittens in from a rescue on the coast of Virginia, near Newport, that flooded because of the hurricane. I'd love to give checkups to the littles."

"Sounds like a great opening day. I'm glad there were no hiccups."

She side-eyed me, and I knew something was up.

"You know how Diana quit on Angelica right after I got the job offer?"

"Yes. I still can't believe she locked up the clinic and just never went back. Angelica didn't find out until the following Monday when she showed up with an angry pet owner standing outside the office."

Daisy laughed. "He was only angry because Angelica didn't show up for work until eleven in the morning. Since the clinic opens at nine, they weren't happy when it was still closed. Anyway, Angelica showed up today demanding both me and Diana come back. She promised us raises, but I know her promises mean nothing. The funny part was when the same client who was waiting outside the clinic on Monday came to me today to have his dog looked at."

The Big Mountain Animal Rescue agreed with Daisy that they should also be a veterinarian to pets and farm animals in the area. They had spent the past three weeks fixing up the barn and the main floor of the house for the veterinarian and rescue offices.

Today they opened for the public.

"I think Lydia was excited. She helped a lot with the landscaping for the farm. She started her landscaping and horticulture business last year, but this was her first big assignment. She loved it. And Sophia baked special animal treats. I told her she should start a business selling them, and she acted as if I told her to chop off her hands."

"How are things with Jackson?" I asked, unsure if I wanted the answer.

She waved her hand from side to side. "So-so. I'm doing a lot of babysitting for him. He won't answer my questions about why he is up at The Blue Spot so often. I joked he must be up there all the time because he's planning to get married, and he went quiet. Has he told you about a girlfriend or someone you think he might like?"

"No. He only talks about hockey or Lucas."

I had noticed Jackson acting strange the past few weeks, but that was his business. I was sure he'd talk about it when he was ready. I hoped he'd open up before anything bad happened.

He saved me from making two of the biggest mistakes of my life. Falling off the wagon and not trying to win back Daisy.

"Speaking of Lucas, I picked up some farm animal books for him, so I thought it would be cute to bring him to the farm and read about the animals he sees there."

I nodded. I had met Lucas several times and understood why Daisy was so in love with her nephew. The little boy was more like her than Jackson.

"We can pick up some pizza on the way. Have a pizza and book party."

She side-eyed me again. "Any excuse for pizza, huh, Cillian?"

"What? Kids love pizza. It's a fact."

"Kids and hockey players named Cillian."

Right as we walked out the door of the rink, I leaned down to kiss Daisy. "You may make fun of my love of pizza, but it was pizza that sort of brought us together. Remember the night you begged me for a slice of my pizza at Joe's?"

"We had met long before that."

"I know, but that was the night that paved the way for our love."

"I don't agree. It was Arizona who brought us together."

"Well, I like to imagine it was pizza."

She threw her head back and laughed, her brown hair catching in the sunlight, causing it to glitter with golden streaks.

"If you had your way, everything would originate with pizza. You'd find a way for the Big Bang to be because of pizza."

My heart swelled in my chest as I studied the happiness on her face. The way her eyes crinkled and her cheeks flushed. She was striking, and I knew in that moment, I'd never let her go.

She gave me a squeeze, and we continued toward her car. With the salary she was making at the rescue, she went out and bought herself a used Toyota Camry. It was three years old but in good condition.

We stopped at her car door, and I said, "I was here when Brian became team captain, and I never remember a tickle bombing. You didn't tell Jackson about how bad I am with tickles, did you?"

Daisy's eyes widened, but she shook her head. "Uh, no. Why would you ask that?" Then she snorted.

Wow. Jackson was right. Daisy was a terrible liar. But she's *my* terrible liar, and I hoped she always would be.

The End

ABOUT ELIZABETH LYNX

Elizabeth Lynx is a *USA Today Bestselling* writer of rom-coms with a lot of steam and characters that cause you to laugh-out-loud.

She has worn many hats in life: mother, wife, photographer, graphic designer, executive assistant, and used to print pictures for the White House. For the past several years, she's put down on paper all the crazy voices in her head. Those voices did some naughty things.

You can learn more about her and her books by visiting her website www.elizabeth-lynx.com